WOLF WHISTLE

Also by Lewis Nordan

Welcome to the Arrow-Catcher Fair
The All-Girl Football Team
Music of the Swamp

WOLF WHISTLE

a novel by
Lewis Nordan

Algonquin Books of Chapel Hill
1995

Published by
Algonquin Books of Chapel Hill
Post Office Box 2225
Chapel Hill, North Carolina 27515-2225
a division of
Workman Publishing Company, Inc.
708 Broadway
New York, New York 10003

First Front Porch Paperback Edition, March 1995. Originally published in hardcover
by Algonquin Books of Chapel Hill in 1993.

Grateful acknowledgment is made to *Story* magazine, where Chapter 1 of this novel
appeared as "Get Well Soon."

"I Just Want to Make Love to You," written by Willie Dixon, © 1959, 1987 Hoochie
Coochie Music. Administered by Bug. All Rights Reserved. Used by Permission.

This is a work of fiction. While, as in all fiction, the literary perceptions and insights
are based on experience, all names, characters, places, and incidents are either products
of the author's imagination or are used fictitiously. No reference to any real person is
intended or should be inferred.

Library of Congress Cataloging-in-Publication Data
Nordan, Lewis.
    Wolf Whistle : a novel / by Lewis Nordan.
       p.   cm.
    ISBN 1-56512-110-4
    I. Title.
    PS3564.O55W64   1993
    813'.54—dc20   93-1011
                                                                     CIP

10 9 8 7 6 5 4 3 2 1

First Edition

For you, Li

The author wishes to acknowledge indebtedness to The Virginia Center for the Creative Arts and The MacDowell Colony, which provided residencies during the writing of this book.

WOLF WHISTLE

1

WHEN SCHOOL started in September, Alice Conroy's fourth graders missed their injured classmate, Glenn Gregg.

Alice had just graduated from the Normal and knew all the latest techniques of modern education. She encouraged the children to talk about Glenn and the accident whenever they wanted to. Alice had come to live with her Uncle Runt and to keep house for him, since her Aunt Fortunata had moved out.

"Don't hold back," she told the children, her fourth graders. "Ask anything you like."

So they said, "Is he dead?" and "Is he still on fire?" and "Am I going to die?" and "Are we all alone in the world?"

Her education was already paying off, Alice thought. See how they opened up? See how inquisitive, how willing to reveal their innermost thoughts and feelings?

She wished she could call Dr. Dust, her old professor at the Normal, to tell him of her success. Last year, when she cried, naked in his arms, he had told her, "There is great pain in all true love, Alice, but we don't care, do we, because it's worth it."

He was right, too. Alice knew that. Love was worth anything, everything, no pain was too great in the service of true love. The problem with calling Dr. Dust, though, was that Mrs. Dust always answered the telephone and called Alice a slut in a loud voice and slammed the receiver in her ear. If Mrs. Dust would only be a little forgiving, Alice thought, they might be friends. They might share many things.

Early in the term, one day during the art lesson, when the children were busy with three-by-five cards and Magic Markers and big safety pins, making name tags for themselves, Alice surprised everyone and made a name tag for Glenn Gregg as well, the child who was injured and had not returned to school.

The minute Glenn's name tag was done, well, somehow, wouldn't you just know it, things brightened up around Alice Conroy's schoolroom. The filthy flaking yellow plaster of the walls seemed to turn to sunlight. The children seemed truly happy for the first time since Glenn stopped coming to school.

Next, Alice looked up Glenn's reading scores from third grade, in the secretary's file, and assigned Glenn to the Bluebirds reading group, just as if he were sitting there among them. She assigned him a desk, too, right on the second row. She put his name tag on it.

And Glenn's name was taped beneath an empty hook in the cloakroom. Glenn had his own "boot bin" for galoshes on rainy days, his own dental hygiene chart on the bulletin board, just waiting to have Checkup #1 entered on it as soon as he returned.

Then Alice got the idea of making Get Well cards. And what an idea it was! It was the best idea anybody at Arrow Catcher Elementary School had had for a long, long time. Everybody had to agree.

Mr. Archer, the vice principal, came down each day and stood in the doorway of the room while the children bent over their construction paper and scissors and Elmer's glue. He beamed, he glowed! Alice Conroy was working out just fine, he was forever announcing in public places. Alice Conroy was a wonderful new teacher, experienced teachers could learn a few things from Alice Conroy. Mr. Archer had a habit of picking at his scalp and making his head bleed.

Every child in Alice's class poured his or her whole heart into the Get Well cards, and each was an object of art. One card showed a brilliant ball of gold glitter, which represented the gasoline fire at the Greggs' home. The gold ball was connected by a long streak of silver glitter to the tiny stick figure of a little girl. This was the artist trying to put out the fire with a stream from a garden hose. The caption said, *Get Well Soon, Glenn Gregg.*

Another child had cut from different colors of construction paper flamelike shapes of red and yellow and orange and black. Behind the flames Glenn's smiling face was visible. The caption said, " 'I'm fine,' said Glenn, 'but boy this fire is hot!' "

Other cards carried simple messages of "I miss you, Glenn" and "I hope you feel better" and "Come back to school soon" and even "I love you." These were decorated with blocky, brick-colored drawings of Arrow Catcher Elementary, and trees and sunshine and fluffy white clouds, and bees that said "Buzz buzz" upon flowers.

At the end of the school day, when the final name had been signed to the final finished greeting card, Alice went down to Mr. Archer's office to use the telephone. She intended to call Mrs. Gregg, though she had been warned by other teachers that Mrs. Gregg was impossible in conversation because of a bad stammer.

Mr. Archer was an athletic man, with a crew cut. He was a family man. He sent out Christmas cards each year with a color photo of himself and Mrs. Archer and their four happy children under the Christmas tree. He had last year's Christmas card blown up to eight-by-ten and framed on his desk. The whole family was happy, you could tell. Alice couldn't help but wish she was one of those children under Mr. Archer's tree, with a big curly-haired doll or a shiny new Western Flyer bicycle for a present.

When Alice came in to use the telephone, Mr. Archer was having a heart-to-heart talk with one of the older children, a sixth-grade boy named Benjamin, with crossed eyes and Bucky Beaver teeth. You just wanted to squeeze him, he was so cute.

Mr. Archer was trying to make Benjamin confess that he had written "Mr. Crites sucks cocks" on the restroom wall. Mr. Crites was the shop teacher. Mr. Archer kept picking his head and examining the blood under his fingernails and talking to Benjamin.

He was asking Benjamin for a writing sample of the offending phrase, but when he saw Alice, he looked up and smiled and motioned to her to go ahead, go right ahead and use the telephone all you want to, no problem, no need to ask, make yourself at home.

Benjamin carefully wrote "Mr. Crites sucks cocks" on a page of notebook paper for the writing sample.

Mrs. Gregg answered after ten rings.

She had a stammer all right, and it was more serious than even strong warnings had prepared Alice for. Mrs. Gregg was saying, "Hngh, hngh, hngh, hngh, hngh," trying to say "hello," but she could not make the word come out of her mouth.

Alice pressed on with her message. The children had made Get Well cards for Glenn today, Alice said, and she wondered whether it would be all right to drop them by Mrs. Gregg's house on the way home from school.

It was no use. Mrs. Gregg was stuttering her fool head off. Now she was saying, "Ynuh, ynuh, ynuh, ynuh." Maybe she only meant yes. Nobody knows.

Alice told Mrs. Gregg that Glenn was very well liked among his classmates, that she knew from his previous teachers that Glenn was a smart boy, and a hard worker, and kind to others, and courageous and loyal, and had many other fine attributes. She took a wild guess and said that he was popular.

Mrs. Gregg declined further comment. Her breathing was heavy with exertion.

Alice said, "Mrs. Gregg, excuse me. Please. All I really need to know is this. Can I stop by your house in the next half hour or so and drop off these cards? It would mean a whole lot to the children."

On the other end of the line, nothing.

Alice said, "If you'll just give me some sign, a signal that it's okay, I'll drop the cards off this afternoon."

Mrs. Gregg continued to breathe hard into the telephone.

Alice said, "If you hang up right now, right this minute, Mrs. Gregg, I will take that for a *no*."

Alice waited. Mrs. Gregg did not hang up.

She said, "Okay, good, good. That's real good. I know where you live, from the school's files. Thank you so much."

MRS. GREGG'S house was a clapboard shack in Balance Due, the white-trash ghetto of Arrow Catcher. Scumtown, it was sometimes called. Even Alice's Uncle Runt, whom Alice boarded with, lived a street or two outside of Balance Due.

Filthy, violent men in shirtsleeves sat in doorways. They staggered, they leered, they drank out of sacks, they worked in muddy yards on junker cars with White Knights bumper stickers. Bottle-trees clanked in the breeze. A hundred-year-old voodoo woman wearing a swastika stirred a cauldron above a fire in a yard nearby. A young man tried to convince a woman, a girl really, to let him shoot an apple off her head with a pistol.

The tiny shack of Mrs. Gregg seemed scarcely habitable. The front yard was utterly without grass. A burned-out car sat like the husk of a huge dead insect in the front yard. All the window screens of Mrs. Gregg's shack were rusted and ripped out, and some of the windows themselves were broken. Shards of glass lay on the ground beneath them.

No one answered when Alice knocked. She pulled open the busted-out screened door and stuck the sheaf of colorful pages behind it and propped the door back in place as well as she could.

Her hands shook, and her step was quick as she hurried away.

The Nazi voodoo woman yelled after her, "Are you the Lard Jesus?"

Alice said, "No!" and started to run.

The voodoo woman hollered after her. "Lard Jesus was a white child."

Alice Conroy hollered right back at her. "And he didn't have tits, either, did he, Miss Smartypants!"

THAT NIGHT she lay down on the narrow cot in her room in Uncle Runt and Aunt Fortunata's house and thought about her old professor at the Normal, Dr. Dust, and the good college life, and peeled the newspaper off the wall by her bed, strip by strip for a while, and then cried her guts out and buried her face in her pillow and said *I love you I love you I love you* and fell asleep. It was all that she could think to do.

A few days later, Alice received a surprising note in the mail from Mrs. Gregg.

Written in a cramped little white-trash script on coarse, lined paper from a Blue Horse notebook, it was an invitation for Alice to bring the entire class to the Greggs' home to visit their fallen mate, little Glenn.

The message was simple: *Come see Glenn. This Friday morning, I guess. Bring everybody, it don't matter.*

This would be the first anyone at all had seen of Glenn since before the accident.

If it were any other teacher on the staff, Mr. Archer declared, he wouldn't allow it, he simply would not. Never on this earth would he allow fifteen nine-year-olds to walk into Balance Due, even in the early morning, no way, not a chance, no siree bobtail. He was making a mistake, he said, he knew it, it was against his better judgment, he shouldn't allow it, he didn't know what was in his mind, he ought to have his head examined.

But he did it. He gave his permission. The class could go and visit Glenn Gregg. "You can go," Mr. Archer said, "but for God's sake, Miss Alice, be *careful*." The visit would be considered a field trip.

On the day of the field trip, Alice called the roll. She assigned a child to erase the chalkboards. She collected the last of the field-trip permission slips and took up milk money and lunch money and workbook money. She announced the winners of the creative writing awards and shushed the children quiet while Mr. Archer made the announcements over the intercom.

Mr. Archer warned all children, grades K through Six, against improper activities in the restrooms, including cussing, smoking, loitering, writing cocksucker on the walls, and standing behind stall doors with a friend.

He led the Pledge of Allegiance, announced the annual airplane turkey drop, gave the date of the next P.T.A. meeting, and said that teachers would be sending home reminders to parents of the Rainbow Tea scheduled for later in the year and that he hoped many would volunteer to help out.

Finally it was time to leave. The weather was not perfect, but it was not terrible yet, either. A strong wind had come up and there were low clouds and a threat of rain. The trees were as bare as skeletons, a little unearthly for so early in the Mississippi autumn.

Fifteen children, little white boys and white girls, followed Alice in a single, wavery line, out the big front doors and down the front sidewalk and across Arrow Catcher, Mississippi, in the direction of Balance Due, where their friend was consumed by fire.

Alice made a game of their walking. "We are a snake," she said, and the children weaved down the walk and caused their single-file line to wriggle like a snake.

They cut down an alley and took a shortcut behind McNeer's Grocery, where Mrs. McNeer, who had once owned a gorilla, kept a big cage with iron bars.

Alice raised her right arm as she walked, and fifteen children's right arms lifted up as well. Dogs barked from behind fences as they passed.

Alice raised her left arm, then, and fifteen left arms raised up. Her arms swayed, and their arms swayed like slender trees. They danced this silent dance along the wide sidewalks.

They passed Red's Goodlookin Bar and Gro., which was a bootleg whiskey store that sometimes kept a loaf of bread and a can of Vienna sausages on the shelves, and Alice looked inside and saw her Uncle Runt there, through the screened door, drinking from a pint of Old Crow. Blues singers were tuning up on the front porch to sing Robert Johnson tunes.

Alice and the children kept on, down the graveled streets, into Balance Due.

A skinny yellow dog dragged a saddlebag full of harmonicas down the street in its teeth.

At the front stoop of the Greggs' house, the line of children broke up, and they moved uncertainly about for a moment, and then they stood clumped together, shy and embarrassed. Alice yanked open the dreadful screened door and knocked with her knuckles against the wood.

Mrs. Gregg opened the door, a tiny, dark little person with a pointy nose and pointy chin. She might have been made of pipe cleaners, she was so thin.

When she spoke, there was a tinny nasality, but, surprisingly, no trace of a stammer. The absence of a stammer was the first thing Alice noticed. Mrs. Gregg said, "Here is the fourth grade! Here is the fourth grade! Right at our front door!"

Mrs. Gregg called back into the house for her own children. "Dougie and Wanda, and all you children, Wayne and Gresham, too!"

They were all ages, the Greggs, when they emerged from the tiny, dumpy recesses of the little house, which smelled suspiciously of petroleum. Wanda, the only girl among them, was fifteen. She was beautiful. Her breasts were full. There was a small scar on her upper lip. Alice wondered why she was not in school.

The others were much younger. Gresham was still in diapers. Dougie and Wayne were not old enough for kindergarten. All of them were pretty, with dark, bright eyes and sidelong grins.

The oddest thing was, Mrs. Gregg was talking. Not just talking, she was yakking up a storm.

She talked about the weather. She talked about the local arrow-catching team, its prospects for the playoffs. She said that she had a black cat that was too shy to come out to meet strangers. She apologized for the meagerness of her home. She hoped the children were not frightened by the condition of the neighborhood, the rubbish and ruined lives.

She asked each of the children to tell her their names, and she made much of each, as if each were especially pretty or interesting. She commented on the children's heights and smiles and clothes. She asked them which subjects they liked best in school and whether they kept pets or had hobbies.

She spoke of more astonishing things, of the difficulty of having a physical handicap, the stammer that she had so recently been silenced by, the loneliness, alienation, the shock of being so afflicted in adulthood.

Then, if that were not amazing enough, she told of marrying young, of her disappointment in marriage, of never having danced with her husband, or any man. She told of her failed dreams of romance and the joyless mechanics of sex.

The fourth graders fell in love with Mrs. Gregg. Alice did, as well.

When Mrs. Gregg spoke, winter scenes, unlike anything Alice had ever actually observed in tropical Mississippi, appeared before Alice's mind's eye. Snow fell through forest trees. One-horse open sleighs jingled along country roads. Chestnuts roasted on open fires. City sidewalks were dressed in holiday decorations. Little hooves clattered upon rooftops. Corncob pipes and button noses would not be suppressed. Toyland Towns rose up around the base of conifers.

On and on Mrs. Gregg talked, and as she did Alice found herself irresistibly drawn to burst into holiday song.

Mrs. Gregg told of the progressive tyranny of her husband, the sarcasm and mockery and intrusions into her smallest privacies. Whenever she spoke on the phone with a friend, Mr. Gregg interrupted to ask who she was speaking to. Finally she had no friends.

He mocked her hill accent, and the color and texture of her hair, her thinness, her height and small breasts, the poor clothes she wore.

And then one day she realized that she was having difficulty speaking. It was a funny thing at first. Even Mrs. Gregg thought so.

She began to speak in clichés. Scarcely a sentence came out of her mouth that was not a cliché. "A penny saved is a penny earned," she found herself saying, often without relevance. "A rolling stone gathers no moss." "A bird in the hand is worth two in the bush." She seemed to have no thought that was her own.

Who could fail to listen? Not Alice. No one at all, not the wiggliest rascal-child gathered in this poor shack took an eye off of Mrs. Gregg. Some of the children reverted to thumbsucking and hair-twisting and speaking in baby-talk. One cried, one wet his pants. But not one child lost interest. They were fascinated. A low, quiet music of humming could be heard, a sentimental silence of carols and holiday tunes.

Mrs. Gregg continued her strange story. The clichés multiplied, she said. She found herself speaking a dead language, she said.

And then something else happened.

The clichés began to overlap. "Don't cross your bridges before they hatch," she said one day. "A bird in the hand gathers no moss."

When this began to happen, she said, Mr. Gregg's rage at her increased. He threatened her; he called her a bitch, a slut, a whore, a cunt.

The children's eyes were enormous. They trembled in fear. They broke into sudden, spontaneous choruses of "Let it snow, let it snow, let it snow!"

She became a hostage, she said. Every mixed cliché endangered her life, and yet she could not stop. "I'm smiling from end to ear." "The worm is on the other foot." "It's so quiet you could hear a mouse drop."

Mr. Gregg began now in earnest to beat her, she said. He bruised her arms, he pushed her down, he knocked out her front teeth with his fist.

It was then, she said, that she lost the power of speech altogether.

Alice said, "But you have it now! You have such beautiful speech!"

Mrs. Gregg said, "Santa Claus comes tonight."

Alice said, "Mrs. Gregg, please!"

What happened next explained many things to Alice, though when it was over even she had a hard time believing it had really occurred. In fact, later in life, Alice often doubted her memory of even the most important details of her own existence, history, and experience, especially her heart filled with hope when she left the Normal, in love with Dr. Dust, let alone this small interim in another family's home.

Much later, when Alice was an old woman, she thought back on this year when she lived with Uncle Runt and Aunt Fortunata, and of the dance she danced with a group of children in a snaky line through snaky lands, of her young love of her professor at the Normal, and the dream that she and Mrs. Dust might somehow, someday, trade places and then be friends, and of the rain-swept Delta, of the poor tar-paper shack and the newspaper-covered walls of her Uncle Runt and Aunt Fortunata, the speechless parrot that lived in a cage in her uncle's house, her year as a schoolteacher, the Get Well Cards Project, the holiday music, the injured child. Even to herself, the memory was improbable.

When she told these tales as an old woman, no one believed her, not even the description of the stammering and stuttering of a pipe-cleaner woman, the impoverishment and pain of so many. "Oh, Alice, you exaggerate everything!" her friends said, these years later, her family, even the children, now all grown up, who had danced behind her in a line. "Oh, Alice, you are just the funniest thing!"

And yet Alice was sure of what Mrs. Gregg told her. She thought if Dr. Dust would just leave his wife, or at least answer his phone, then he would believe her, too. She said *I love you I love you I love you* into her pillow at night for many years, and into the chests of many naked men as well, and always it was only Dr. Dust.

Mrs. Gregg said, "Glenn poured gasoline, Glenn poured gasoline, right on his daddy's bed; he was trying to burn up his daddy, when he burned up hisself instead."

Now Alice understood. By thinking of the tune "Here Comes Santa Claus" Mrs. Gregg could speak without stammering. With that tune in her head, she could say anything. Santa Claus had broken her chains and set her free.

Alice was born again. She saw the ancient star rise over Bethlehem. She saw shepherds abiding, flocks and myrrh and miracles in the dunes. She saw what was unimaginable, classrooms in the swamp with black faces and white faces together, singing, "Jump down, turn around, pick a bale of cotton." She saw children holding hands with grown-ups, black and white, singing "We Shall Overcome" in long lines and in churches. She saw a church bombed in Montgomery, dead children, marchers in Selma, freedom riders in Jackson. She saw bombs flying over the miraculous desert, Baghdad burning, Emmett Till dead, Medgar Evers dead, Martin King, the little blue figure of her own still-born child, years hence, herself an abandoned child as well, names, faces, geographies not yet known to her, for in the extremity of her pain and need, linear time disappeared and became meaningless, blood running alongside lost hope in the streets of many nations.

Alice suddenly knew she would never see Dr. Dust again, or only once more, to prove something, to prove that love is a cruel dream, and not worth the pain and that we are, all of us, alone.

Alice said, "Oh God. Oh my God."

IN THE next room, little Glenn Gregg was lying in an iron bed with a thin mattress. The room had been painted since the fire, but black traces of it still streaked the ceiling, and all these months later the room still smelled like a furnace.

The bed was the only piece of furniture. An electric cord with an exposed light bulb at the end of it hung from the center of the ceiling. The burned child would never recover, this much was clear immediately, and for the first time. Glenn Gregg would soon be dead if he was lucky.

Alice and the children followed Mrs. Gregg into Glenn's bedroom. The bandages were gone. Glenn's face and arms and bare little chest were visible above the crisp sheets. He was unrecognizable as himself, or even as a child. His scars were like taut ropes. His hair was gone, everything. His eyes were wide open because the lids had been burned away. His teeth were white and prominent as a skeleton's, because he had no lips.

Mrs. Gregg touched a white cotton handkerchief to the mucousy hole that had been his nose. She took a bottle of eye wash from her pocket and applied a few drops to each eye.

There was nothing to say. Alice and the class stood for a while in silence.

All around the little bedroom, Scotch-taped to the walls, were the Get Well cards that the children had made. The sunny colors, bright fires, the kind sentiments, the bees that sang "buzz buzz" from the yellow petals of crayon flowers. *Get Well Soon, Glenn Gregg.*

After this, everyone moved out of the room, silent, shuffling. No one spoke.

Then Wanda Gregg, the fifteen-year-old sister, said to Alice, "I'm getting married."

They were standing in the bare, poor living room now. Glenn's breathing was ragged behind them.

What could anyone say?

Alice said, "Well, that's fine. That's just fine, Wanda."

Wanda said, "He advertised for a wife in the personals in the *Memphis Press-Scimitar*."

Alice said, "Is he—is he older than you?"

Wanda said, "He's forty-something. He has a cattle ranch in Missouri. That's what he says, anyway."

Alice said, "These things work out, Wanda. He will love you."

Wanda said, "I'd have to go in any case."

Alice said, "Oh, Wanda."

Wanda said, "Well, thank you for coming to see Glenn. It was nice meeting you."

The Greggs stood on the porch and waved.

The schoolchildren formed their single line behind Alice. They wound through the gravel streets of Balance Due. The bottle trees, the woodsmoke, the boy with a pistol and an apple and the crying girl, the Nazi voodoo woman, Red's Goodlookin Bar and Gro., and all the rest.

They did not speak. They did not dance. They made their way back towards Arrow Catcher Elementary School, where they would move through the hours together in safety, in silence, before it was time to go back to their homes.

It was still early in the day, not quite noon. The rain had started now. Alice thought of Wanda Gregg and the rancher in Missouri who was waiting for her, forty-something. She saw pastures filled with horses, salt licks on fence posts, troughs of water, mangers of dusty oats. A child tied to a dying farmer.

Dr. Dust was more like fifty-something, and he wasn't really waiting, he had a wife, and no ranch. He wasn't even answering his telephone.

And did it really matter that Santa Claus had restored a mute woman's voice, and her hope in this world?

Alice had to get out of Balance Due while it was still safe to move along the roads with these children. They walked quickly, one step at a time, without looking from side to side. Violent men were awake now, cursing whores in the rain-drenched street.

2

THE DAY Glenn Gregg's daddy got back from New Orleans was the same day Lady Sally Anne Montberclair decided to park her big white Cadillac out in front of Red's Good-lookin Bar and Gro. and leave the motor running and scoot inside, out of the first drops of rain, on an errand. Glenn's daddy was named Solon.

Solon was a skinny man, with thin, greasy hair. He had been sleeping in his clothes for six months to protect himself from creatures in his mattress, gabardine pants that were baggy in the butt and a western-style shirt and a bolo tie, brogans on his feet. Solon considered himself a ladies' man.

It was early September, still hot as blue blazes in Arrow Catcher, Mississippi. Now this rain! The Delta was steaming. The colored school hadn't even started up yet—the white school started the week before—and so there were kids standing around up on the big front porch of Red's store, colored children, teasing and messing, all time messing, their parents would say, flirting with each other and playing grab-ass, when Lady Montberclair showed up.

Bobo, he was the center of attention, always was, fourteen years old, fote-teen he pronounced it, always into something, always had him a joke going, a dare, something another, some kind of mess, all time messing. Wore him a white shirt, too, like a natural man, Bobo did, not no feed-sack shirt neither, uh-uh, Bobo had him a tie knotted up at the collar, tied it his ownself, four-in-hand, something another, and a wide-brimmed felt hat pushed back on his head, and a big-ass gold ring look like a walnut on his finger, "Italian gold," Bobo said, out on the porch of the store, "Eye-talian" he pronounced it. Bobo was a spote, sho now, what you say.

Bobo, he's saying, "Who want to look at my lizard," that's what he's saying, be making little girls out on the porch squeal, sho was, and little boys be saying, "All time talking about lizard, uh, uh, uh," and all he's doing is be showing off a picture of his Chicago girlfriend, which he carried in his wallet, a white girl, lizard-skin wallet, bought it down to Mr. Shanker's Drug Store, right in Arrow Catcher, but how do they find a lizard big enough to put your money and your pitchers in, is what Bobo wished he knowed. Actually it wont no picture of his girlfriend, it was a picture of a movie star, Hedy Somebody-another, Bobo don't care, Bobo he'd say most anything, make somebody squeal.

He had a couple of the kids fooled about the movie star, too, the one he said was his girlfriend. Bobo said, "That's some good white stuff." The little girls squealed and covered their faces, and the boys burned with envy, even those who didn't believe him for one minute, they said, "All time talking about tail."

A couple of guitar players were there, too, black men, out on the porch this morning, sitting in cane-bottom chairs with their big boxes, blues singers, singing Robert Johnson tunes, just to wake themselves up a little bit. Robert Johnson was the King of the Blues, that's what people said. Robert Johnson grew up right down the road from Arrow Catcher, down in Morgan City, got hisself killed, long time ago, by a jealous husband. Don't that seem like just the way the King of the Blues ought to check out of this life? Blues singers like those on the porch revered Robert Johnson, they liked to start their day playing Robert Johnson tunes.

One of the singers sang about waking up in the morning and seeing the blues walking like a man. He sang, "Come on, blues, take my hand." This was Blue John Jackson singing, he was a big man. The other man, he didn't sing, the albino. He had pale, pale skin and white nappy hair and split lips. He didn't hardly talk. He wore him some dark shades, day and night, because his eyes was pink. He was just called The Rider. Sometimes he put down his box and blowed on his harpoon, he had about four harps, all different keys.

Everybody was scared of The Rider. Wouldn't nobody

talk to him. Everybody said The Rider had pink eyes like a grave rat. Everybody said The Rider had done been brung back from the dead by a hoodoo woman name of Lily.

Bobo looked at The Rider. Bobo said, "Uh-huh." Bobo had this little smirk. He pushed his hat more back on his head. The Rider was playing "The Preaching Blues" on his guitar. Bobo walked right up to him. Bobo said, "Hey, Rider, you's a mysterious motherfucker, ain't you." The little girls squealed. The little boys said, "You crazy, man, you crazy, you all time talking about mysterious."

Anyway, here come Lady Montberclair, just when Solon Gregg come blowing back into town from New Orleans wearing gabardine pants and plenty of Wildroot Cream Oil. All Lady Montberclair was wearing this early in the morning was a canvas trench coat and a pair of bedroom slippers. Leastways, that's the way it looked to Solon Gregg, who was interested in this sort of thing, like the ladies' man that he was. Lady Montberclair was bare-legged and rumored to be modern.

Well, when did you wake up, girl, goddamn! Look at you, coming straggling out of bed, ain't done scratching yourself and looking like the unmade bed you just straggled up out of! Law-zee, Lady Montberclair! White lady's hair looked like it hadn't never been combed, long and blond and falling down across her shoulders like some kind of

movie star. She wont wearing no makeup, eyes looking
like a raccoon, make you want to kiss her right on the
durn mouth.

Solon ran a steel comb through his hair, which had just
grown in after the house fire six months ago. Solon hadn't
set foot in Arrow Catcher since the fire, hadn't seen his
wife or children since then, neither. Armed robbery was
Solon's trade, though he was not adverse to other honest
work either, you know, extortion, for example.

Well, Sally Anne Montberclair she was a good-looking
woman, there wont no doubt on this green earth about
that, now was they, she did have a nice turn of ankle,
sho did. That's what Solon Gregg was thinking just at the
same time he was taking a little taste with the boys for old
time sake.

Runt Conroy, he was standing in Red's place, too, like
usual. Runt looked like a weasel, with real beady eyes,
and wore a felt hat with a grease stain on the crown. He
looked especially bad lately, since his wife had done left
him, Fortunata, and run off to Kosiesko. Runt's niece Alice
had come to look after the children, so that was good,
didn't interfere too heavy with his drinking. Runt had Fortunata's phone number in Kosiesko, down on the coast,
funny-looking durn number, too, if you asked Runt, just
in case of an emergency, but he was scared to call her up,

she might hang up on him, and besides that he didn't know who might answer the phone, and, anyway, what bigger emergency could there be than your wife running off and leaving you, and Fortunata already knew about that, didn't need to be told.

Runt wore the hat pulled down over his eyes like Humphrey Bogart. Runt figured he might be a happier man if he had him a good strong name like Humphrey instead of Runt. Cyrus was Runt's real name, but nobody never called him that, never had. He was the smallest of the children in his family, when he was a boy, and his daddy always called him "the runt of the litter." It stuck, wouldn't you just know it.

Runt slipped his half pint of Early Times into his jacket pocket, out of sight. He turned away from the vision of Lady Montberclair in her man's trench coat, in gratitude for many things, and focused his attention on other things, things that didn't scare him quite so much as them raccoon eyes and blond hair, the Royal Crown box, the half-empty shelves in Red's store, a bin full of black bananas and half-rotted peaches, a scrawny chicken in the meat case. That chicken looked like the victim of a lynching.

Another patron of Red's, the housepainter Gilbert Mecklin, was on hand, with his blind daddy, Pap. Gilbert always wore white painter overalls and a paper cap with Curry

Lumber Yard printed on it, and he smelled like paint and turpentine and Aqua Velva shaving lotion, in addition to the whiskey.

Gilbert opened up the meat cooler and took a big knife off the butcher block and sawed off a hunk of rancid cheddar from the wheel. Then he took his old blind daddy, who always wore aviator sunglasses with green-tinted lenses, out in back of the store to look at a hellhound Red had lassoed down at the town dump when it was half-grown and brought home for a pet.

Pap said, "Can you pet it?" Talking about the hellhound. He held onto Gilbert's arm like a child.

Gilbert said, "Feed him that hunk of cheese first, see don't he warm up to you a little."

Out on the porch the colored children were messing. They were giggling. They were talking trash. They were saying, "I dare you, I dee-double-dog dare you."

The blues singers were singing a song about the devil knocking on their door. Blue John Jackson sang about greeting old Satan like a natural man. He sang, "Come on, Satan, take my hand."

Solon Gregg still had his eye on Lady Montberclair, him being a ladies' man. He raked his steel comb through his hair, and felt the teeth of the comb on the raised scars left in his scalp by the fire. His head was still tender.

Solon was about to say something to Lady Montberclair,

he was about to call her by her given name, Sally Anne, see
could he make her squirm, when two things happened that
shut him up, good and proper.

The first thing was, Lady Montberclair spoke first, before he could open his mouth. She was talking to Red about
a purchase. Red owned Red's Goodlookin Bar and Gro. He
stood behind the counter. Red was old and freckle-faced
and his hair, which stood straight up on end, was mostly
white now.

Lady Montberclair said, "Red, I know I'm intruding
here, and I'm sorry, honest I am, but it's an emergency. Do
you carry tampons?"

The truth was out about Sally Anne Montberclair: she
was modern.

The rain that had threatened to fall all morning began
to fall in earnest now, plink-plink-plink, on the porch roof
and on the tin hellhound shed out back.

Rufus McKay, a sixty-year-old colored shoeshine boy,
woke up in the shoeshine chair from a dream of electrocu-
tion and sang the chorus of "Danny Boy," and slept again.
The pipes, the pipes are calling.

Pigeons fluttered in the rafters, nervous.

The blues singer, out on the front porch, sang about
walking with the devil side by side. He sang about beating
his woman till he gets satisfied.

The fact is, Red did carry tampons, and sanitary napkins, too. He kept them beneath the counter, wrapped up real careful in butcher paper, like plain white Christmas presents. He just never had sold a package of feminine items to a woman before. He kept a bone-handled .44 pistol right beside them, so he would always know right where it was.

Usually men bought Kotex. A man knew how to purchase a box of Kotex. A man would whisper a discreet word to Red—like, "The Crimson Fairy's visiting my house today, podner, can you do a little something to help me out?"—and Red would slip him what he needed, like contraband, to be smuggled away.

This was the first time a woman had ever asked Red for such of a thing.

At first Red didn't say nothing. He only put both his hands down on the countertop and stared far away into the distance. His jaw jerked with a small convulsive twitch; he might have been having a seizure of some kind. Red was not believed to be a well man. Some people said he ought to go on and retire and maybe take himself a Florida vacation.

Then, without ever looking directly at Lady Montberclair, Red reached up under the counter, beside the big pistol, which he nudged to one side of the shelf, and pulled out a small, wrapped package and placed it on the open space in front of him, between the jerky and the jug of pickled eggs.

The lithesome Lady Montberclair fished her wallet from

the pocket of the trench coat she was wearing, and started
to take out a half-dollar piece to pay for her purchase.

The blues singer on the porch sang that he had to keep
moving to stay out of the path of the blues, he sang that the
blues were falling all around him like hail.

The children on the porch were daring and double-dog
and dee-double-dog daring Bobo. They said, "Axe her, you
so smart. Axe her, you like white stuff so much."

The blues singer sang that there was a hellhound on his
trail, a hellhound on his trail.

Red said, "No charge."

Lady Montberclair looked at Red. She said, "No charge
for Tampax?"

Red didn't want to be making change over no box of
tampons. He already like to been had a stroke.

He said, "It's all taken care of."

Red wished he hadn't said this. He didn't want to seem
to say that the tampons were on the house. That didn't seem
right. Or that one of these old boys standing around here
was buying it for Lady Montberclair, like it was a drink.
"Compliments of the gentleman at the end of the bar." That
wasn't right, neither.

Lady Montberclair said, "But that's silly, Red. Here."
She placed the half-dollar on the counter.

Red didn't know what to do. Making change was out of
the question.

He said, "Thank you."

She said, "Is that enough?"

He said, "This is what it costs."

She said, "Exactly? Is there any tax?"

He whispered, "Lady Montberclair, *please*."

She said, "Oh, all right. Thank you, Red. Much obliged."

Blue John Jackson sang, *Hellhound on my trail, hellhound on my trail*.

So that was the first thing that kept Solon Gregg quiet for a few minutes, what Lady Montberclair said. It looked like nothing else was going to happen. Even Solon Gregg was finding it hard to speak to a woman who had just paid hard cash for tampons and on her face wore the look of a woman who meant to use them, as advertised.

Solon raked the steel comb through his hair one final time and something, who knows what, a sudden effluvium of Wildroot, maybe, or some unwashed, hair-borne contraband from New Orleans, flushed a pigeon out of the rafters.

Red said, "Solon, keep that durn comb in your pocket, these pigeons got a right to roost here, too." He took the comb out of Solon's hand and put it up under the counter with the Kotex and the .44.

Solon had it in his mind to follow Lady Montberclair out onto the porch and tell her he could use a ride into

Balance Due in that fine white Cadillac car of hers, if she didn't mind. It'd be okay with Solon if the niggers out on the porch got the idea that him and Miss Sally Anne were together, friends, you know.

In fact, they might could be friends. Solon was so lonely right now, anything seemed possible, or at least hopeful.

He pictured himself sitting up in that wide front seat with her, big as Ike and twice as natural, and calling her Sally Anne, right to her face, and liking it, too, and then her dropping him off in front of his own house, where his fool wife and murderous children would be watching out the window.

But then a second thing happened that stopped him.

Hole up a minute, spotey-otey, what's going on here? Somebody else had done come into the bar and gro., whut the hail?—the spotey little colored boy from out on the front porch, po-itch Solon pronounced it, wearing a man's hat on his head and looking to purchase two cents worth of Bazooka bubble gum, with the comics inside. Just whut in the durn hail?

It was Bobo, of course, who else is it gone be, that durn Bobo, acting on some dare another, double and dee-double and dog. Somebody out on the porch, ain't no telling who, done bet Bobo a nickel he wouldn't axe that white lady for a date, since he liked white girls so much, since he's all time carrying on about a white girl, toting a white girl's picture in his wallet, axe her Bobo, go on and axe her, you so smart, you such a spote.

Red watched the little nigger go to the wire rack and pick two pieces of bubble gum out of an open box—you had to watch a nigger like a hawk, anybody'd tell you that much, they'd steal you blind, rob your chicken house and your back pocket and your gold tooth in one easy motion, what a nigger'd do—when all of a sudden Bobo turned around and looked right square in Lady Montberclair's face.

Well, sir.

He said what he said, Bobo did.

The blues singers had already stopped playing. They must have heard the children talking, must have suspected that the boy from Chicago didn't know no better.

Lady Montberclair didn't even hear him say it, what he said, or the other neither, didn't seem like. She just stood there while Red put her already-wrapped-up tampons in a brown paper bag. It took him a minute, his hands were shaking so bad, not from anything Bobo had done, just only from making this bizarre sale to a woman.

Seem like Red didn't hear the spotey little boy neither. Red said, "Y'all come back," to Lady Montberclair. Now what'd I say that for, Red wanted to know. The last thing on earth Red wanted was for Lady Montberclair to be coming back into his store again, acting modern.

Lady Montberclair said, "Much obliged," again. She was on her way out the door.

Everybody else heard it, though, what that spotey little shine did, dared to have did. Runt Conroy sure heard it. Runt heard it and wondered if he could teach his parrot to say hubba-hubba. His parrot couldn't say a word, only sound that durn retarded parrot could make was a noise like a cash register. Maybe it could learn hubba-hubba.

Gilbert Mecklin heard it, the housepainter, just about the time he was helping his blind daddy come back up the steps. Gilbert didn't have time to pay it no mind, but he heard it. Heard him whistle, too. Wolf whistle, real low.

Pap said, "Are you sure that's a hellhound? To the touch it seemed to be built more like a rat."

Gilbert said, "Well, it'd have to be a moughty big rat to get mistook for a hellhound, Pap."

Rufus McKay heard it, in his sleep, and sat up real sudden in the shoeshine chair and sang, "Pardon me, boys, is that the Chattanooga Choo-Choo?" and slumped back down and slept again.

The pigeons moved about on their perches in the rafters, restless.

Solon Gregg heard it, too, the man of flames.

Solon said, "What did you say?" Speaking to the spotey colored child.

He said this slow and deliberate and mean.

Probably nobody in Red's Goodlookin Bar and Gro. knew that history was about to be made, well, I mean, how could they?

One of the pigeons in the rafters, bout that time, he took himself a good long shit, oh boy, felt good, whew, cleaned his old bird-guts right out, sho did. He turned to another pigeon, sitting up in the rafters with him, he say, "You sleep?" Other pigeon said, "Naw." Pigeon say, "Look at that child, the little nigger, the one what got him two pieces of Bazooka in his hand." Second pigeon say, "Uh-huh." Pigeon say, "That boy, now he's surprised, he surprised he-ownself, you better believe it." Second pigeon say, "Is?" Pigeon say, "That boy he thank he most be talking to he-ownself, just loud enough, you know, to satisfy the dare." Second pigeon say, "Do?" Pigeon say, "Look like to that little spote somebody be reading his mind." Second pigeon say, "Maybe I was sleeping after all. I ain't shore I'm keeping up with this conversation."

Solon stepped between Lady Montberclair and the door, blocking her way out.

He said, "Hole up, Miss Sally, jess one minute, tell we get something straightened out cheer."

Lady Montberclair could not get past without touching Solon, so she stopped.

Solon said to the child, "Why don't you jess wipe that grin off your face, boy, and tell us yore name?"

The child said, "Huh?"

The front porch cleared off, blues singers and children and all.

Solon said, "Don't you know how to talk to a white man?"

The boy said, "I own no."

Solon said, "Yew own no."

Red was watching all this from behind the counter. His white hair was sticking up like chicken feathers. He said, "Solon, let me pour you a little taste, son, you bout to need a little taste, ain't you?"

Lady Montberclair said to the boy, "Come on here with me, Junior, walk out to the car with me and get in the backseat, I'll drive you home."

Solon kept the door blocked with his body, and so nobody moved. He said, "I don't thank so. Not tell this here boy tells me his name."

The child said, "Bobo."

Solon said, "Bobo."

The child said, "Yeah."

Solon said, "Yeah." Solon said, "Where-bouts do you live, Bobo?"

The child said, "Chicago."

Solon said, "Chicken in the car and the car won't go, that's the way to spell Chi-car-go. Right?"

Bobo said, "Huh?"

Solon said, "That's two *huh*s and a *yeah*, Bobo." He said, "Where do you stay?"

Bobo said, "Uncle."

Solon said, "Listen here, Bobo. I want you to apologize to my friend here. I want you to apologize to this here white lady." He motioned his head in the direction of Lady Montberclair. He said, "I want you to say 'I'm sorry' to this here good-looking white lady in her raincoat."

Lady Montberclair said, "Bobo, you go get in the car, right this minute. I mean it. I'll drive you home."

She pushed her way past Solon Gregg, out the screened door, and so then Bobo slipped through, too, in the instant of daylight between Solon and the door, and flew down the porch steps and jumped in the front seat of Lady Montberclair's Cadillac.

Lady Montberclair got in the car in a hurry and didn't wait for directions, she just drove away, towards a section of Arrow Catcher called the Belgian Congo, or sometimes just Niggertown. That's where she thought Bobo must be staying, she didn't catch on right away that Bobo's uncle lived out on Runnymede.

As the Cadillac pulled away, Solon turned back to the

other men in the room. He said, "Settin up in that-air front
seat like Cock-of-the-Roost."

Solon said, "Did you hear him out on that front porch,
bragging about white women? Seem like I heard him say he
was carrying a pitcher of a white woman in his wallet. Did
anybody else hear him say that?"

Red's hair stood up straighter and more electric than
usual. He said, "Well, now, welcome home, Solon, welcome home from the big N.O., boy, the Big Easy, the Land
of Dreamy Dreams. Tell us all about it, son, have a little
taste of Old Charter with the boys, Solon, why don't you
now. Let me crack you open one of these half-pints, do you
some good, settle your nerves. Still Happy Hour, so the
Co-Colas are free." Happy Hour was early in the morning
at Red's Goodlookin Bar and Gro.

Gilbert Mecklin, the housepainter, took out his half-
pint again and uncapped it and chased down a snort of
Four Roses with a little bit of Co-Cola. Gilbert had heard
that New Orleans was below sea level and that all the
graves were above ground. He said, "What about them
durn graves, Solon? How do they dig a durn grave *above* the
ground, is what I'd like to know. I never did understand
that. Runt, you ought know something about this, in your
line of work."

Runt Conroy had dug a few graves in the Delta, there

was no doubt about that, guilty as charged. He dug graves before there was machinery to dig graves with, when it was only a pick and shovel and zinc buckets on a rope to haul out the dirt.

It was odd to Runt, though, that until right now, this minute, grave-digging had never seemed like a morbid occupation. Never a thought about who was going in the hole, or what would happen to them once they were down there.

You'd think it might have troubled him from time to time, preparing final resting places. He had known some of the occupants of those graves, too, plenty of them, over the years. These weren't faceless corpses to Runt, they were citizens of Arrow Catcher, Mississippi, his hometown.

He dug his own mama's grave, not too many years ago, with a backhoe. She died of a broken heart because Runt was such a failure in life. No woman could live long in the knowledge that her son was the gravedigger and town drunk in the sorriest little podunk excuse for a town in the sorriest state in the nation. That's why she died, who wouldn't?

That's what the funeral parlor director told Runt before his mama's body was washed and prepared for burial. The funeral director's name was the Prince of Darkness, nobody could account for just how this came to be so. The Prince of Darkness was a mean little baldheaded man and had been called by this name since he was a child. All those years with this name might have had something to do with his personality and choice of occupation.

Dr. Hightower, down at the free clinic, said, "Don't believe it, Runt, your mama didn't die of a broken heart, the Prince of Darkness is a madman, there is no telling what that baldheaded old fool is going to say next, your mama died of an aneurysm, plain and simple, and the Prince of Darkness ought to be locked away forever for saying such a durn thing."

But Runt halfway believed the Prince of Darkness anyway. Broken hearts made sense to Runt Conroy.

Still, there was joy in life, in the face of death. Runt loved to dig a grave on a backhoe.

The backhoe was a huge machine, enormous, and the sound it made when the shovel, the bucket it was called, engaged the face of the planet with its teeth and dug in and leaned back on the stabilizers and heaved back on the crane-bar and erupted from the earth full of dirt and caused the engine to strain and diesel fuel to blow out of the exhaust manifold like a fire-breathing dragon and to sound like a tornado coming through town. But that was not the way Runt thought about it. It was not power and fire that Runt Conroy thought about when he considered a backhoe.

The backhoe was operated from the driver's saddle by a series of tiny yellow levers with little black balls on the tips.

Pull one—just a touch, just the smallest hint of movement with your fingertips—and the stabilizers, the "stabs" they were called, lowered into place beneath the big machine, and the machine lost substance and weight and became like musical notes from a xylophone rising up into the air, accountable to no one, ascending from the ground upon the stabs, as if those tons of steel beneath Runt's steel saddle were as light as air, lighter, as if the machine were a hot air balloon rising up over a deserving town, and Runt could imagine that he dangled beneath its substancelessness in a wicker gondola, in a completion of silence, a mote on the ambiguous breeze.

But today, suddenly, when Gilbert said this to him about graves in New Orleans, something ended for Runt, some innocence, or blindness, fell away from him, and Runt Conroy suddenly knew what he had not known before, that he was all alone in the world, that we all are, and because he had put off knowing this simple fact for so long, he was also as defenseless as a child against the random and irrelevant terrors of the solitude as well.

Maybe this is the reason Runt believed that he had to follow the spotey child in the white Cadillac into the Belgian Congo and lay eyes on the floor where he walked and on the roof that sheltered his head.

Runt said, "I got to be going."

Red said, "You got to be going?"

Runt said, "Yeah, I'm taking off."

Red said, "It's still Happy Hour."

Runt said, "I know."

Red said, "You ain't mad at me, are you?"

Runt said, "Naw, Red, I ain't mad, I just got to be going, is all. I'll be back."

Red said, "So you're saying you just got to be going."

Runt said, "Right."

Red said, "And you ain't mad."

Runt said, "I ain't mad."

Red said, "You're a rambling man, am I right, Runt? You're like the Robert Johnson tune. You're a rambling man."

Red considered Runt his best friend, him and Gilbert Mecklin. Red said that Runt Conroy and Gilbert Mecklin, the crazy housepainter, were the two best friends a man could ever have. Red said he couldn't stand it if Runt was mad at him, or Gilbert neither one.

Runt said, "Now you're talking, Red. I'm a rambling man. That's it, that's all."

Red said, "Don't never leave me, Runt."

Gilbert Mecklin said, "He ain't mad at you, Red, course not. He won't never leave you."

Pap Mecklin said, "That hellhound's snout felt a lot like a rat."

Gilbert Mecklin said, "It ain't a rat, Pap, it's a hellhound. It's too durn big to be a rat. It's as big as a collie dog, how's it gone be a rat?"

Pap said, "I own no, but that snout felt moughty like rat snout. And I notice it sholy did gobble up that cheese."

So Runt left the store, didn't know why his ownself, just woman's intuition, he reckoned, except of course he wont a woman, what in the world did that expression mean anyhow, it wont logical. He thought he might just take him a little walk, wont the craziest thing anybody ever done, now was it, take a walk? He mought just take him a little walk down towards the Belgian Congo, nothing wrong with that, mought just do that, see could he run up on the boy's folks, that'd be all right, wouldn't hurt nothing.

He was walking in the mud now, down the middle of the Congo road, Esequeena Street. The rain was falling pretty good now.

Runt called out, "Uncle." This was the name he remembered that the child had spoken. "Oh, Uncle." Sometimes you could just holler up a nigger.

The streets of the Belgian Congo were not paved, not even gravelled, some of them. The streets were lined with shacks. The only trees were chinaberries, stunted in a ditch.

He didn't know which house he was looking for, he just kept on trying. "Oh, Uncle, come out cheer."

Nobody was out on the street. Most of the shacks had crumbling chimneys, and even on a warm day like today, white smoke from the cookstoves hung above the chimneys like the smoke was too indolent, too heavy, too oppressed, something another, or maybe just too durn lazy and dispirited to make an escape.

He said, "Uncle, you here?"

The rain kept on. Runt was getting pretty wet now, soaking in pretty good.

Occasionally Runt saw a black face peeking out a window, and then the face quickly disappeared, when it saw his own white face. Nobody wanted to help him. Well, why would they? He might be a bill collector.

The rain picked up some now. Runt was beginning to smell like a farm, or a world war. These were his wife Fortunata's frequent accusations, and he carried them with him wherever he went. Runt looked at the rain on his arms, and it seemed to be steaming in the heat.

Chose him a house, don't know how he come to choose this one, clapboard so gray it looked like silver in the new rain, don't know why, just looked like a good place to scrape mud off your boot.

He hollered out, "Somebody come out cheer." Now he scraped mud off the other shoe and stepped the first back down in the mud. He said, "Durn," said this to hisself. He hollered, "Looking for Uncle."

Didn't nobody come out, and Runt couldn't see nobody neither one, but then a disembodiment answered him, he reckoned that's what it was, old woman's voice through the closed door of the house.

Voice said, "Ain't no Uncle."

Runt spoke with ease to disembodiments. He said, "Where is he at?"

Voice said, "He daid."

Runt said, "Naw, he ain't dead. He got a boy staying with him."

Voice didn't speak.

Runt said, "Out-of-town boy, name of Bobo. Sharp dresser, play the fool."

Voice didn't speak.

Runt said, "Can you tell me where I can find him?"

Voice said, "I own no."

Runt said, "Boy got a piece of white trash mad at him."

Voice said, "You?"

Runt said, "Naw, not me." Why'd she want to point out a thing like that?

Runt looked up and down the muddy street, hoping to catch sight of Lady Montberclair's white Cadillac car, but he knew it was hopeless, she was long gone.

Runt said, "Does Uncle stay down here?"

Voice said, "I thank he stay on Runnymede. I thank he farm shares for Mr. Tootie."

Runt said, "Uncle don't stay in the Belgian Congo? He stays on Runnymede?"

Voice said, "You ain't gone hurt him, is you?"

Runt said, "I ain't gone hurt nobody."

Voice said, "He don't stay in the Belgian Congo, naw-sah."

Runt said, "Well, okay. All right. Much obliged."

Just then, the front door of the house opened up, and a girl about nine years old came out. Behind her, a long, skinny black arm materialized from nothingness and poked out of the dark shack to try to grab her back inside but too late, that little ninny was already out on the porch, sassy, what you talking bout.

Runt said, "You know a boy name of Bobo?"

The girl said, "You ain't posed to be in the Belgian Congo."

Runt said, "You know Uncle?"

The girl said, "You smell like bird dooky, all the way up on the porch."

Runt stopped. He said, "I do?" He said, "You can smell me all the way up on the porch?"

Voice said, "Come back in this house, Doe Rinda."

Runt said, "My wife says the same thing."

Voice said, "I'm own give you a switchin put you in an inch of yo sorry life, chile."

Runt started out, down Esequeena Street, out of the Belgian Congo. He needed a drink, that's what Runt really needed.

Runt was walking hard now, slogging through the mud, wringing wet from head to foot.

Then a thought came to him like a voice. The voice said, *You are drinking yourself to death with violent men.*

He missed his wife, who had done left him and run off to Kosiesko in the Nash Rambler, even left all the children behind. He thought about the song The Rider and Blue John had been singing, *hellhound on my trail, hellhound on my trail*. He tried to remember how he had fallen into the necessary business of digging graves.

Happy Hour had done passed long time ago by the time Runt got back to Red's Goodlookin Bar and Gro. Red set him up with a free Co-Cola anyhow, he was so glad to see him, sho was.

Runt woke up Rufus McKay, in the shoeshine chair. He said, "Rufus, do I smell like birdshit to you?"

Rufus lurched up out of his sleep and sang a few lines of "Pennies from Heaven." He slept soundly again.

Red said, "Who told you you smelled like birdshit, Runt?"

Runt said, "Gal down in the Congo."

Red said, "Well, niggers got a keen sense of smell."

Runt said, "I got to confess to you, Red, that piece of ridiculous information don't give me much comfort."

Red's hair was standing straight up. He said, "I ain't claiming to be no anthropologist. You ain't never heard me claiming to be no anthropologist, is you? I never made no such claims. I am just merely reporting some well-established scientific facts that I happen to have in my possession. They ain't no need to snap at me. I just wish you wouldn't take science so durn personal, Runt. Like the poet said, ain't no need to kill the messenger boy."

Runt didn't answer, he was thinking about something else.

Red turned his attention to Solon Gregg. He said, "Solon, you're mighty quiet, boy. It's not a good sign in a man."

Solon said, "Give me back my durn steel comb."

3

A WROUGHT-IRON fence ten feet tall surrounded the Montberclair property. Through the fence Solon could see a driveway that curved around back and out of sight, and cobblestone walkways lined with ferns. The house itself had an elaborate adobe look to it. Solon thought a whole tribe of Mexicans might as well be living there. To the left stood a fountain with water spilling out of some fool concrete animal's mouth.

Solon grasped the bars of the fence with both hands and put his face up to the opening between them. The trees above him were old and big and were hung with long gray beards of Spanish moss.

There was something just slightly too Mexican about this place, it seemed like to Solon. Seemed like, any minute, somebody might be jumping out at him and jabbering his head off in the Mexican tongue about tortillas and jumping beans, habla-habla.

He felt the weight of the pistol in his pants pocket, and he put his hand on the heavy mass of it, for comfort. It was one thing to pull a gun on a queer in New Orleans and roll him for a blowjob and his money and his suit, but

Solon couldn't quite picture himself holding a gun on Lord Poindexter Montberclair.

He took out his steel comb and raked it once through his hair and tidied himself up a little and felt better.

Actually, Solon had no notion in his head of robbing Lord Montberclair in the first place. Well, perish the durn thought! He might try to extort a few dollars out of him, sell him a little information, maybe, but he didn't have no thought of robbing him.

Solon was in the driveway now, unsteady on the cobblestones. The white Cadillac was not in the driveway, but Lord Montberclair's little El Camino was, the little red hybrid of car and pickup truck.

Lord Montberclair surprised Solon. Scared the shit out of him, more like it. He stepped around a bend in the cobblestone path, from behind some big fan-shaped ferns, and said, "Hold it right there, Mister. State your business."

Lord Montberclair had been a captain in the army, served in Korea. He had his pistol drawn and aimed straight at Solon's head. The pistol was a German Luger, solid black, and Lord Montberclair held it out at arm's length, with ease. He looked like somebody just itching for an excuse to shoot somebody else's brains out.

Looking back on the scene, Solon could imagine it going worse than it did. He could have gone for his own pistol, which would have taken five minutes at least to pull out of the pocket of his blue gabardine pants—the hammer always got snagged in the fabric—and Lord Montberclair, in his calm, savage way, could have squeezed the trigger on that dangerous-looking Luger and shot Solon straight in the face and then blowed the smoke off his gun barrel and walked back up to the house and called Big Boy Chisholm, the town marshal.

What happened, though, was this. Solon regarded the pistol in his face with mild interest. He placed his finger alongside his nose and blew snot onto the cobblestones, left side, right side, and then wiped his finger on his blue gabardine pants and left a silver streak of mucous in the fabric, just below the lump his pistol made where it was outlined in his pocket.

The barrel of the pistol that Solon was looking into was like a long tunnel with the meaning of life inside. Deep in the tunnel Solon saw what the queers in New Orleans must have seen when they looked into his own gun barrel, a long permanent darkness.

Solon said, "Morning, Mr. Dexter. I was about to despair of raising you this morning. I just dropped by with some information, won't cost you a red cent."

The Luger stayed pointed in his face. Solon said, "It's about your wife, Sally Anne."

Lord Montberclair lowered the pistol to his side.

He said, "Has something happened to her?"

Solon looked past Lord Montberclair's face, over his shoulder, as if to say, "Well, I notice she ain't here and you don't seem to know where she's at."

Lord Montberclair raised the pistol again.

He said, "Tell me what you know, trash."

Solon did not shrink from the pistol. He raised his hands slowly out in front of him, palms up. He said, "I ain't trying nothing funny." He reached around, real slow, with his right hand to his left pants pocket and slipped out the steel comb. Solon always felt better about himself, no matter the circumstances, if he knew his hair was in place. He held the comb up in front of his face for a second to identify it. Comb, that's all.

He dragged the comb through his hair one time and then slipped it back in his pocket.

He said, "I wouldn't mind setting down with you and scussing this like two gentlemen, Mr. Dexter."

Lord Montberclair lowered the pistol a second time.

He said, "But Sally Anne is all right, isn't she?"

Solon said, "Me and Sally Anne are close, I won't deny it. We're friends. That's my deep feeling. I want to protect her like a brother. I wouldn't think of charging a penny in this world for any information I might have, neither. That's just the way I am, protective of innocence and beauty, I won't apologize for it."

Lord Montberclair said, "Come on in the house, Solon. Do, please, won't you? And pardon my manners, please. Uncalled for, quite uncalled for. I haven't been myself lately. Now just what is the story here? What is going on? Help me get this straight, won't you, please. Tell me everything you know about Sally Anne. And listen, Solon, I'm sorry, very sorry indeed, about that cowboy business with the pistol, really I am. I shouldn't have done that. And the name-calling. I didn't mean a thing by it. Not a thing. My nerves are not good these days, you understand. Truly I haven't been myself."

Solon noticed that Lord Montberclair had not put his gun away. He carried it in his hand with him into the house, dangling down at his side.

They sat together on one of the sun porches in wicker chairs with cushions decorated in Mexican scenes, adobes and red sand deserts and cactuses and purple donkeys and big yellow suns. The Mexicans made Solon uncomfortable, and there were as many trees indoors as there were outdoors, it seemed like.

Lord Montberclair brought a silvery percolator full of fresh coffee from the kitchen and set it on a glass-topped table, along with two cups and saucers and containers of sugar and cream.

This scared Solon for a minute, when he thought that

right out of the clear blue sky he might have to drink a cup of straight coffee, without no warning whatsoever. But then Lord Montberclair set out a bottle of brandy as well, and poured a big dollop of it into his own coffee and then offered it to Solon.

Solon said, "Much obliged to you, Dexter. You are a fine man, a gentleman and a scholar, you truly are."

Solon told Lord Montberclair what he knew. He emphasized that this information was absolutely free, it wouldn't cost Lord Montberclair nothing, not a red cent.

Solon didn't leave out the part about how Sally Anne was dressed. He apologized profusely for having to mention such things, the sturdy cotton duck of the trench coat against the flesh of her bare calves, the wide bare V at her throat and chest.

When he got to the part about the child Bobo riding in the front seat of the car with Sally Anne, Solon grew cautious. This whole thing could backfire on him.

He said, "I know Sally Anne must of had her reasons, good reasons, too, for inviting that buck up in the front seat with her. I didn't question that part one minute, no sir."

Lord Montberclair was red-faced from coffee and brandy. He wagged his head slowly from side to side.

He said, "I don't know, Solon. I just don't know."

Solon let the silence hang between them for a long time.

Solon said, "I hope you won't feel no compellsion to pay me nothing for this information."

Lord Montberclair looked up now, as if he had not heard.

He said, "I didn't know that you and Sally Anne were close." He shifted the Luger in his lap.

Solon didn't care much for the way this sounded.

This was a tricky business, no two ways about it.

Solon said, "Close? Well, now that's a good one, ain't it? You're not only a smart man, Mr. Dexter, you're comical, too. Close? Me and Miss Sally Anne? Are we talking about the same two people? Whoo! That's a good one, all right. Me and Miss Sally Anne—close friends! Now that'll be the day, won't it! Wake me up for that one, I want to see it my ownself!"

Lord Montberclair said, "You said you were close. You said she was like a sister to you."

He was switching the Luger's safety catch on and off, on and off.

Solon said, "Oh, I see what you mean, now I see the mistake here. I done misspoke myself. I done left a false impression, if that's what it seem like I said. Sho did."

Lord Montberclair said, "Are you close or not?"

He shifted the Luger from one leg to the other, clickety-click with the safety.

The strain of this interview was beginning to wear on

Solon now. He sensed that he was out of his element, and that there was no money in the venture in any case.

He said, "Miss Sally won't hardly speak to me, Mr. Dexter. Won't look in my direction."

Lord Montberclair said, "I distinctly heard you say you were close friends."

Dexter drank straight out of the bottle of brandy now.

"You said she's like a sister to you. That's what you said."

Lord Montberclair was very nervous. He was flipping the safety on the trigger guard, on and off, on and off, click-click-click-click-click.

Solon was astonished to find the truth coming out of his mouth before he could stop it.

He said, "I got me a sister in St. Louis, Mr. Dexter, baby sister name of Juanita, call her Neat, run off and married a nigger pimp and set up for a ho and broke our mama's heart, you can imagine, called me up one day and said she's about to die she's so happy, she's so much in love with this nigger pimp, and she's so glad to be out of Mississippi, she said she's got this little nigger baby, little boy, and me his onliest uncle in the world. Onliest woman in the world I'd die for, Mr. Dexter. I miss her so much I want to die sometimes, so instead, I go down to New Orleans and roll queers, killed one of them, maybe, I don't know, probably did if I could remember it, and all I'm thinking about is,

What's done happened to me, what's going to come of me, too proud to go see my own little sister and my own baby nephew, what's ever going to come of me?"

Lord Montberclair said, "So you were lying. You're not close to my wife." ·

Suddenly Solon was able to lie again, and his life became more manageable.

He said, "No, I just meant she put me in mind of Juanita, my little Neat, my own sister. That's all, that's all I meant to say. Not that Miss Sally Anne is married to a nigger pimp. I didn't mean that."

Lord Montberclair stopped clicking the safety of the pistol. He seemed satisfied.

He said, "You've suffered other troubles as well, I understand. Something about a fire? One of your children injured? I've been meaning to ask about the tyke."

Solon was astonished at what had just happened. He almost never thought of Juanita. What in the world got into his head to tell all that stuff about Juanita?

He put his fist up to his mouth and gave a little cough.

"Scratchy throat," he said. "I think it might be an allergy."

Lord Montberclair poured three inches of brandy into Solon's coffee cup.

Solon fingered his pistol through the gabardine. Its small heft provided some comfort.

He could get it out, too. It wasn't impossible. Not quick draw, but he could get at it. You wouldn't have to be quick with Lord Montberclair, drunk as he was.

Solon could work the pistol out of his pants pocket, a little at a time. Dexter would never notice. He could have that little pea-shooter in his hand before Dexter ever knew what happened. He could blow this arrogant rich man's hair and eyeballs all over these ferns before he knew what hit him. That's what he was going to do, too, if Lord Montberclair wanted to pursue the subject of Solon's white-trashery any further. Lord Montberclair wouldn't look half so handsome, with all his military and plantation airs, if he had a bullet between his eyes, now would he?

Sometimes in New Orleans Solon didn't even remember the men he robbed. Sometimes he would wake up the next morning with folding-money in his pocket and new suits in his closet, and maybe a wet dick in his pants, and not know where he got any of them. He might have killed somebody and not remembered, he honest to God couldn't be sure. He hoped he left at least one of those perverts bleeding in a hotel room.

Solon wouldn't mind killing Lord Montberclair, either. It would give him pleasure, sholy would. All Solon wanted to do right now, though, was just to get out of this durn crazyhouse alive.

The conversation was over at last. Nothing was decided.

Lord Montberclair said much obliged for the information, thank you very much, you are a good neighbor, words to that effect.

Solon said, "No payment necessary, none at all."

Lord Montberclair said, "You're a good man," and paid Solon nothing, stingy son of a bitch.

After Solon had walked back out into the rain, Dexter Montberclair filled up a whiskey glass with ice and poured bourbon over it—it was late enough in the morning to switch from brandy to bourbon now—and sat down again in a wicker chair on the sun porch. He stretched out his legs in front of him and propped the glass on his stomach.

His lips were numb with alcohol. For two months now, Sally Anne had been sleeping in the room she called her office. It was an insult to Dexter. A woman was supposed to sleep in the bedroom with her husband. Wasn't she? Wasn't that the deal when they got married? Didn't a woman promise to sleep in the bed with her husband, when they spoke their sacred marriage vows?

The last time they talked, Dexter said, "Why, Sally Anne?"

Sally Anne said, "I don't know."

He kept on asking the same question.

All she would say was "I don't understand it myself, Dexter. I've just got to be alone for now."

Well, what kind of answer was that?

When Dexter stood up from the wicker chair, he wobbled a little bit and realized that he was drunk.

He left the glass of bourbon on the table and stuffed the Luger into the front of his pants. He started to walk through the house, though he wasn't sure where he was going, and he felt unsteady on his feet.

If that sassy little nigger lived out on Scratch Ankle, Dexter's own place, it would be a different story. He'd evict them, whole family, simple as that, cut off their credit, anyway. That was the whole problem with letting foreign niggers come into town. Our own niggers don't act like that. It's these out-of-town niggers that are forever causing the trouble.

Dexter had seen the light revolver in Solon's pocket. It might as well have had a string of Christmas tree lights on it, it was so obvious. You could all but read the writing on the barrel.

This was who Dexter found himself indebted to.

Dexter was pacing the house. Sun porch, living room, kitchen, and back again. He adjusted the gun in his pants for comfort.

His head was beginning to clear up. He needed a clear head, to think what he had to do here. He had to do something. He might just pistol-whip the shit out of his wife, it's what she deserved, humiliating him like this. It might give him some satisfaction.

He paced through the kitchen and looked at the dishes Sally Anne had left in the sink. She must have gotten up in the middle of the night and fixed herself a snack. A plate with crumbs on it, cookies maybe, the last of a pan of brownies, and a glass that had had milk in it.

Why didn't she tell him she wanted a snack? Why didn't she come out to the bedroom and wake him up? He would have been glad to fix her something to eat, to bring her milk and cookies down to the room where she was sleeping, for that matter. All he wanted was for his wife to be happy.

Dexter was crying now, and adjusting the pistol in his pants. Why wouldn't Sally Anne just allow him to make her happy? He wanted to take care of his wife, to baby her, to make Jell-O for her when she was sick, and tapioca pudding, and to feed it to her with a spoon, and then to sleep next to her. They could work something out, couldn't they, if they just loved each other?

SOLON GREGG didn't know what kind of reception to expect at home. Not so good, probably. Probably nobody at home was going to be overjoyed to see him, he might as well admit the truth about that, right up front.

He had left in a hurry six months ago and hadn't been in touch since. Still, he sometimes let himself hope that things would be different. Why didn't he wish for a million dollars, while he was at it?

Solon thought about the Prodigal Son, that sleazy, lazy-ass rich boy in the Bible. It pissed Solon off to think about him. Maybe that's the way some rich sissy's daddy acts when you spend all his money and run his good name in the ground, chasing off from home in a big car without no insurance on it and living in a pig sty in some unfriendly city in a foreign land.

Shit. Goddamn. Must be nice, that's all Solon had to say about it, must be durn nice. "Daddy, look, I done spent every cent you give me and been rolling queers in New Orleans and living in a stinking room in the District where the former tenant was still laying dead in the bed in the room with me, blue as a fuckin Andalusian rooster, when I paid my cash deposit to the landlord and helped him pull the dead sumbitch out in the hall by his feet. I been fucking fatted calves and wearing they clothes and spending they money on food and drink a swine wouldn't never eat, ever since I seen you last."

Oh, I'd just love to see that, Solon thought. Yeah, that's the story that would assure me of a proper welcome home, now wouldn't it. I can just hear myself telling my daddy that story when I was a boy. I wonder what kind of reception I would of got if I had come back home with a story like that. I never would have got that ridiculous story out of my mouth. I never would have made it up the front steps, with a story like that on my lips.

The truth was, if Solon had been the original Prodigal Son, Solon's daddy never would have noticed that he was gone, let alone that he had come back home. Solon's daddy would have been too busy trying to get his hands up underneath Juanita's shirt to feel her breasts in the kitchen while she was crying her guts out and trying to fix something for the old pervert's dinner. And Solon's younger brother, who stayed home and sacrificed his whole life trying to keep their daddy from fucking Juanita, would have shot Solon in the heart with a deer rifle for running off in the first place. It's a lucky thing the Prodigal Son didn't have a younger brother like Solon's, he would have got his ass blowed off. The Prodigal Son got lucky twice, if you wanted Solon Gregg's own personal opinion.

Solon thought about that old song, "If I knew you were coming I'd have baked a cake." Solon liked that song, he really did, it was hopeful, it was upbeat and gay, you know, but in a way it made him think about his daddy pinching his sister's nipples in the kitchen. It kind of made him want to throw up. "Howdja-doo, howdja-doo, howdja-doo!" Snooky Lanson and Giselle McKenzie, singing like a couple of songbirds, just warbling they hearts out on *Your Hit Parade*.

Solon wished somebody would bake him a cake, hire him a band, grandest band in the land, and be waiting for him and smiling and happy to see him when he come back home from wandering in a foreign land and living an unfortunate life in a pig sty.

That's what he would do for Neat, too, if she ever came back, his sister Juanita, even if she brought her little nigger child and pimp-ass husband with her, he didn't care. Well, he cared, but he'd just be so glad to see her.

In fact, he'd love to see that child. He'd bake that child a big durn cake. Children loved cakes, he bet. Chocklet. He'd bake that little nigger kinfolk of his a big chocklet cake, if he knew how. He could find out how, he could look up a recipe, buy him some ingredients down at Red's, and a bowl and a spoon and a pan to cook it in.

And he would try to find something in common with the pimp, too, Neaty's husband. What did nigger pimps like to talk about? he wondered. He could tell him about rolling queers in the Quarter. Well, Solon wasn't sure about that, but he would think of something.

Solon had listened to some extra delightful tap dancing on the radio when he was down in New Orleans, tippity-tippity-tappity-tappity, whoo! Whoever was doing that toe-tapping could dance like a motherfucker. Fast, too, lickety-split. Niggers liked to dance, even pimps. Hell, yes! Solon would talk to Neat's husband about dancing. Well, sure. See? That was just the thing! That was just great!

Mainly, though, he'd take Juanita in his arms and hold

her so tight to his chest that neither him nor her would never be lonely again, and she wouldn't never have to remember her daddy's hands on her body. He'd say, "Neaty, baby sister, howdja-doo, howdja-doo, howdja-doo!"

But what kind of names were Snooky and Giselle, anyway? Well, Snooky wasn't bad. He knew an old boy name of Snooky Butler, had a place out in Cohoma County. Snooky let Solon go pig hunting in the big woods one time, long time ago. Snooky was all right. He let Solon use his .32-20 to hunt with. But Giselle? No way, man. He didn't want nobody name of Giselle baking him a cake, not if he could help it. If I'd of knowed you was coming I'd of changed my name, is what Solon wished Giselle McKenzie would sing to him.

Solon didn't expect no cake when he got home today, that much he was certain of. Solon figured he'd be lucky if anybody was civil to him. His wife hated him, his children were scared of him, some of them. The last time he saw his own house, he was jumping out through the window with his clothes and hair on fire, headed for the bus station. His oldest boy, Glenn, had tried to set him on fire with gasoline.

Solon had heard from several different sources now that Glenn, his murderous child who was so handy with a jug of gas, had gotten his ownself singed in the same fire he started. Well, Solon didn't want no innocent child to be hurt in a fire, of course, but at the same time, didn't it really just sort of chap your ass to no end when somebody tried to murder you, even your own son?

I mean, didn't it really just serve the little bastard right, in a way, getting scorched in his own fire? Ought not nobody pour gas on a drunk man and strike a match and then fail to get some signal that it was an inappropriate thing to be doing to your daddy, is all Solon meant, that's all he had to say. So he wanted to keep his homecoming expectations low. That was the main thing. He was trying to be realistic.

BALANCE DUE, the white-trash ghetto, ran right into the Belgian Congo. It looked about the same as when he left, except that it was fall now, late summer. There were no trees here, only house after house, shack after shack, all the same, on both sides of one long straight Delta road.

Power lines swagged from post to post, high above the muddy street, a fragrance of creosote, released from the posts by the rain, always heavy on the warm breeze.

Solon Gregg walked on, in the direction of his house.

On top of each light post, high above the street, perched a buzzard, many buzzards, one right after another, post by post, down the road, as far as you could see, to the railroad tracks, an enormous flock that slept at night in a cypress swamp not far away and came out to sit on posts with heavy-lidded eyes by day. The big birds were slick and black with rainwater where they sat with hunched shoulders and wattled necks like sad old men in dark coats.

The locals called them swamp eagles, sometimes just eagles, though they were clearly buzzards. The birds were descendants and remnants of an ancient flock, attracted here long ago by the corpse-stench of a Civil War battle, when Balance Due and the Belgian Congo were only a big field, a significant Mississippi defeat. Cannon shells and belt buckles and maybe a finger joint still turned up, from time to time, in the muddy street after a hard rain.

These birds were a part of the glorious history of the South. They were written up, now and then, in local newspapers, and in newspapers all across the state of Mississippi. Photographs taken almost a hundred years ago by anonymous photographers with big, boxy explosive cameras and tripods and black drapery over the photographer's head, and recent photographs as well, some in color, stood behind glass in display cases in the Old Capitol Museum in Jackson.

Historians studied the century-old photographs and even named the birds in the flock. Schoolchildren from all around, every county of this sovereign state, as it was always referred to in political speeches, visited the museum in Jackson, and even visited this dangerous street in Arrow Catcher, on field trips, to view the historical vultures, to learn something of their solitary nature, their weight and length, their wing span, their reproduction cycle, their incredible longevity.

Some of the birds on the light posts beneath which Solon Gregg trod on his way home were as ancient as the historical battle itself, older, ninety, a hundred years old, a few of them, so historians and ornithologists reported, and so, as part of this same flock, those birds on the light posts above Solon Gregg had actually fed on the flesh and eyes and tongues and nutritious organ meat of Confederate troops, fallen, hungry, frightened boys before they were made buzzard bait by a mini-ball or cannon shot.

Historical experts identified, with some certainty, several of the very birds in those early photographs. They pointed to dim details of broken-and-rehealed wings, or unusual posture, or mutations of feathering. They looked through binoculars, or they even drugged and carried individual birds away to scientific laboratories in Jackson and Biloxi and spread them out on stainless-steel tables and poked at them and said, "See the similarities between this bird and Bird Vardaman in Photograph Seventeen-A, upper right quadrant, grid-number Thirty-six? It's him all right."

The buzzards were named Vardaman and Bilbo and Hugh White and J. P. Coleman and Ross Barnett and other names of past and future governors and senators of the sovereign state of Mississippi.

Other birds on the light posts, youthful by comparison, possessed only blood-memories of the ancient feast, genetic egg-yolk longings for distant, unremembered culinary ecstasy and freedom from deprivation, and sat with hope in their bird hearts and nothing at all in their bird brains, for many years, decades really, a human lifetime and longer, above the homes of damaged rednecks and maniacs with pistols, on smelly light posts planted in stinking mud, whiling away all of their valuable, irretrievable daylight hours and years in the sad innocence of poultry-patience during this lean century since the glorious Festival of Dead Rebels long ago, and they were content for now with roadkill.

The vulture named Ross Barnett, ancient and ugly, had excellent eyesight. Far away in the distance, at the lucky spot on the rails where the Katy crossed the Dog, Ross Barnett espied an armadillo, not moving.

Ross Barnett closed in prayer his heavy-lidded buzzard eyes and sucked swamp air inside his lungs to savor the fragrance of loss.

Where had they come from, the tribe of armadillo, this gift, this manna, this perfection of the South, sweeter than turtles?

Ross Barnett didn't like to be greedy, he was as good-natured and open-minded and as willing to share the riches of Mississippi as the next old buzzard, but with an armadillo, well, no, he didn't think so, he thought maybe it would be best for all concerned, best for the flock, really, not to do that, not just now, and it wasn't entirely selfish, either, it was just a better idea for him to head on over towards the cypress swamp as if he were calling it a day, and then, when the others were settled in, sucking in swamp poisons with their sleepy, vulturely snores, he would circle back around to the crosstracks of the Katy and the Dog and discover just what sweet surprise this little armor-backed Delta dumpling had hidden away from him, deep inside the shell.

SOLON GREGG arrived at his home. The window was still busted out, where he had, six months ago, jumped through, in flames. Shards of glass still lay on the ground.

The little house where he had lived out the tragedy of his adulthood was the same, and yet he hardly recognized it. It seemed larger, brighter.

He didn't bother to knock, he walked right in.

Wanda, his fifteen-year-old daughter, was the first person he saw when he entered the house.

She was holding a straw broom in her hand, which she dropped onto the floor with a clatter, the instant she saw him. She was terrified of him. She gathered her long shirttails up in both her hands and wrung them like a wet rag.

Solon had forgotten how beautiful she was, how grown up. She was wearing bright blue pedal pushers and one of his old shirts with the long tail not tucked in. Her hair was longer, he noticed, and she had it drawn back in a ponytail and secured with a wide rubber band. She looked like a real teenager, the ones you heard about on the radio and saw pictures of in the newspaper and watched on the TV sets owned by queers in New Orleans.

He saw the fullness of his daughter's breasts and was filled with gratitude that he had never touched her, as his father had touched his sister Juanita.

The younger children ran into the room and hugged him, and said, "Daddy, Daddy!" He knelt down to greet them.

Mrs. Gregg came into the room then, from the bedroom. She did not speak, of course.

Wanda, the teenaged daughter, was still paralyzed with fright, where she stood. The broom still lay on the floor where it had fallen.

Solon did not know how to ask forgiveness.

He said, "Where's Glenn?"

The question was so innocent that choirs of angels in heaven must have begun to sing when he asked it. He knew nothing of his son's terrible injuries.

Solon's wife and daughter, and even his two infant sons now looked at him as if he might be a man from Mars.

Where's Glenn? they seemed to say. *Did you actually say that? Where's Glenn? Are you serious?*

Solon said, "I ain't mad. I deserved it."

He ran his hand once through his hair, to make a small joke about his burns, the fire-fed and sudden baldness he had experienced as he flew through a closed window.

He tried to make his voice sound light and friendly, despite the attempted murder and the violence that led up to it.

Every word out of Solon's mouth produced on the faces of his wife and children a profounder expression of disbelief.

He said, "I reckon I do got me a little bone to pick with him."

Mrs. Gregg said, "Y-y-you don't know, you really don't know, do you?"

Solon stood up in the middle of the floor, with a little smile on his face, like a dim bulb. As he stood, he picked up the two children in diapers and held them, one on each hip.

He said, "Know what?"

He looked first at his wife and then at each of the children in his arms. He tried to keep his dim-bulb smile from fading away altogether.

Mrs. Gregg said, "Oh, Solon, what has become of us?"

Slowly, he squatted and set the two children in diapers down on the floor. He could not hold them any longer, he was afraid he might faint and drop them.

When the children were on the floor, they did not move away, but only held to their daddy's legs without speaking.

Solon said, "He's not, I mean, is he . . . ?"

Mrs. Gregg said, "No, he's alive."

For the first time, she came near to Solon, and took his hand.

Glenn was in the next room, she said.

Solon was like a man waking up after long sleep. He recognized now the clean, fresh aroma of paint in his nostrils. The rooms had been painted, since the fire. In his mind's eye he saw geese running across a yard and beneath clean linen on a clothesline, he saw himself as a boy, whistling in the pale moonlight past the graveyard.

Mrs. Gregg led her husband in the direction of the dying child.

The whole family went into Glenn's room and stood beside his sickbed. He was propped up against two pillows, lying on a clean mattress with crisp white sheets in an iron bedframe.

Oh, Lord. Solon had no idea. Oh, my Lord.

For a long time they only stood there, looking at the dying child. Solon was grateful his wife did not kill him on sight. He looked at the child's scars, the lidless eyes.

From a corner of the room, Solon took up the tattered, cheap-ass, cardboard case that held his Sears and Roebuck guitar, the instrument that had first belonged to his rapist father, and then to himself.

Solon held the guitar across his knees, secured around his neck by a heavy, old, sweat-stained leather strap, which

Solon's father had used to beat Solon when he was a child. He sat in a straight-back chair.

Solon's clumsy left hand went up and down the frets of the guitar neck, seeking the few simple chords of the Blue John Jackson song that Glenn had once loved. His right hand, which for six months had become more accustomed to holding a pistol than a guitar, strummed and picked at the wire strings across the hole of the guitar.

In her lap, propped at a forty-five degree angle, Mrs. Gregg held a zinc washboard. She had brought it in from the kitchen. It was the same scrubboard, with dried soap scum in the runners, that she used with a bar of hard soap to scrub her family's clothes clean of dirt and color in a Number 2 washtub.

On each of the fingers of her right hand, like five strange and dangerous wedding bands, were affixed the washboard picks, with which she transformed the appliance of her kitchen and back porch and aching back into a musical instrument. When she drew a pick sideways along the runners in a certain way, it emitted hornlike song and tone.

Wanda, the beautiful daughter wearing her daddy's shirt, held her strange instrument between her spread-out legs, where she sat, flat-footed, in her chair. It was a washtub from off the back porch, no different from the one that her mother leaned over on washdays, in the kitchen in the winter, on the back porch in the summer, round, zinc, with handles on either side, except that between Wanda's feet it was turned upside down and some additions had been made to it.

A wooden broomstick had been sawed off to half its original length. A strand of piano wire was affixed by a steel staple to the top of the shortened broomstick, and the other end of the wire ran through a hole in the center of the washtub and fastened to a ten-penny nail on the other side. This was a one-string bass.

Wanda propped the free end of the broomstick against the raised rim on the bottom of the washtub. She could tauten or loosen the length of piano wire by raising or lowering the broom handle, and when she plucked the wire with her fingers, she made a deep and rich and metallic music of *thoom thoom thoom thoom*, to accompany her father's guitar.

And so that is what they did now, the three of them, while the babies watched, this family together for the next to last time. They played "Bo Peep," the music of a black man named Blue John Jackson, who lived just a mile down the road.

Solon started pumping his knee and stomping his foot, "One and a-two and a—" Wanda and Mrs. Gregg usually came in somewhere around seven or eight, and so now that is what they did, sooner or later, as the spirit moved them, and as Solon picked through the first high notes on the terrible old rattletrap guitar, and then countered them on the bottom end with strumming.

He said, sang, "Bo Peep . . ."

The guitar went *plink plink*, up high, went *glum glum*, down low.

The washboard went *a-rattle-bing-bap*.

The washtub and broomstick went *thoom thoom thoom*.

Solon said, sang, "Done lost her sheep . . ."

Rattle-bing-bap.

Thoom.

"Done lost her sheep . . ."

Plink.

"So she come trucking . . ."

Bing.

"Back on down the line."

"Bo Peep. Done lost her sheep. Done lost her sheep. So she come trucking. Back on down the line."

The Greggs played and sang in this way for an hour before they quit. It was the only verse they knew, maybe the only one there was.

4

OUTSIDE THE window of the schoolhouse, the rain tap-tap-tap-tapped on the metal slide out on the playground and moistened the dust, which, through the open window, smelled like a fragrance of the sea. The children were gone now. Alice was alone in the schoolroom.

On the metal slide the rain was jungle drums. In the trees it was incantations in foreign tongues.

Alice considered that she had never heard anybody talk about their sad life before. She admired Mrs. Gregg for this, and for not complaining.

Alice put on her raincoat, a clear plastic number she had picked up at the Low Price Store, the latest thing, Mr. Kamp told her.

This would be the last big rain of the summer. The big rivers, the Yazoo and the Tallahatchie, would turn red with the iron oxide of the clay that washed down from the hills in the adjoining counties.

The smaller rivers, Quiver and Bear Creek and Big Sand and Fear God and Yallobusha, would turn black and boil up over their banks and flood the chicken houses and the Negroes' cabins and maybe a cotton gin or two and send water moccasins out of the swamp shallows and up the

sewers. Daddies would go off and drink whiskey in the turkey woods, and mothers would say to their children, "Run
to the Frigidaire, sugar, and get your ole mama a cold Falstaff, and don't forget to open it, dumplin, they's a church
key in the knife drawer, Law, this rain is working on my
last nerve, I swan."

Alice walked out of the schoolhouse. She was living with
Uncle Runt, looking after the children, since Fortunata
left. She pretended like it was a real home.

She wished she was married to Dr. Dust. What good
would that do? She didn't know, it might be an answer.

She was walking now, past the big field where the high
school arrow-catching team practiced in better weather.
Her nephew Roy Dale, Runt's oldest son, was on the team
this year.

Raindrops formed on the clear-plastic raincoat and rain
bonnet. Some of the water ran off her coat in little streams,
and other drops only hung in their places against the plastic, like fat, puffed-out, transparent little crystal sparrows
on a limb.

Alice walked past the crabapple tree on the corner, the
chinaberry tree on the next, the backyard where Mrs.
Stowers had kept a cow when Alice was a child, and where
Alice walked for glass bottles of raw milk for her daddy,
after her mama left town, and before Alice went to live with
her grandmama. She walked past the fishhouse.

Alice didn't see much of anything today, until she passed by the house of Lord and Lady Montberclair.

And even then it was not the stucco house she saw, or the trees or the fountain.

In one of the little crystal balls of rainwater on her sleeve, just as she passed this fine house, she did see something, though.

Alice hadn't even meant to be looking at the drop of rain, let alone looking *into* it. It only lay there before her, on her sleeve, perched like a million other drops of rain. In it, Alice saw the image of a child in the river, some river, running water, anyway. She thought the child must have drowned.

Her eyes would not hold to the spot. She looked away quickly, and then, when she looked back, she couldn't locate that particular raindrop again.

Water collected in the little, turned-up bill of her rain bonnet, and the bill flipped down and emptied a small splash of water into her face.

She wiped her eyes with the back of her hand.

When she got home, Runt's parrot was making its ringing sound, a big African, with green feathers and a yellow beak and a bright red throat and tail.

She checked the parrot's feeder pan and removed the soiled newspaper from the bottom of the cage and put in new.

She put her face up to the parrot's cage and said, "I love you, I love you, I love you" several times, but the parrot ignored her, he would not learn to talk, so she gave up.

Alice imagined Dr. Dust now, at home with his wife. She saw him in a big cracked-leather chair, with his feet propped up on a leather ottoman, his wife near him in a rocking chair. They were surrounded by books, up to the ceiling. She saw that Dr. Dust's wife loved him and so this made Alice sad.

The first of Uncle Runt's children arrived home from school then.

Roy Dale was fourteen. His skin was very white, with big copper-penny freckles.

He walked up to the parrot's cage and put his face up to the bars. He said, "Pussy is good, pussy is good."

Roy Dale missed his mama, he would never say so. He resented Alice.

Alice said, "If you're doing that to get my goat, it's not working."

Roy Dale kept his face in the bird's cage. He said, "Pussy is good, pussy is good."

Roy Dale was wearing a strung bow across his chest and back and a small quiver of arrows on his hip.

Roy Dale said, "I wish we had a cat, so it would eat this parrot."

Alice said, "You are so mean."

Roy Dale said, "I one time heard about a cat that ate a parakeet and then after it did, the cat could talk."

Alice said, "A cat that could talk?"

Roy Dale said, "All right, don't believe me, then."

Alice said, "Screamer McGee, out on Scratch Ankle, came home from the war with a steel plate in his head and got struck by lightning and could get TV on his glasses."

Roy Dale said, "That's not true."

Alice said, "It's as true as a cat that can talk."

Roy Dale said, "Which war?"

Alice said, "Hitler."

Roy Dale said, "They wont no television after that war."

Alice said, "Maybe it was Korea."

Roy Dale said, "Screamer McGee don't wear glasses."

How did Alice get herself into this fool conversation, anyway?

Roy Dale gave her a look, like: *duh*. He turned back to the parrot.

He said, "Pussy is good."

Alice said, "Roy Dale, you wouldn't know what to do with a piece of pussy if it flew up and hit you in the face."

She was sorry she had said it the minute it was out of her mouth.

Roy Dale looked up at her, hurt and surprised. He turned away from the parrot's cage and walked past Alice without speaking, on his way back to his own room. He had to straighten the bow slightly so it would go through the hall door without hitting.

Alice called to him, "Roy Dale, I'm sorry. I don't know why I said that."

He didn't answer, he only closed the door of his room and stayed inside.

After a while, Alice heard a hard, hollow sound of *thunk* on the inside of Roy Dale's door. She was scared to look. She hoped the arrow wasn't sticking all the way through the door.

She hollered down the hall. "Roy Dale, you could put somebody's eye out!"

The rain was still falling.

Runt came home, then, a little drunk. He was wet and smelled like chicken houses. With him, out of the meat case at Red's Goodlookin Bar and Gro., he had brought a scrawny little naked chicken, wrapped up in white butcher paper and tied with a string.

Alice kissed Uncle Runt on the cheek and took the wrapped-up chicken from him. It wasn't much of a home, but it was a home. Alice was grateful.

Uncle Runt walked over to the parrot's cage and stuck his face up to the bars.

He said, "We are all alone, we are all alone, we are all alone, we are all alone."

Alice took the fryer to the kitchen and cut it up into

pieces and dropped it in a pot of water to boil. She took celery and onions out of the refrigerator. She checked the flour bin. Maybe she would make biscuits, too.

Then the other children started to come home, too. Cloyce and Joyce, the twins, were ten, two little blondes. They had a trick of speaking in unison.

They spoke at the same time into the parrot's cage. "Eugene Brister kissed his sister, kissed so hard he kissed a blister," they said to the parrot many times, then giggled their heads off. Eugene Brister was a boy in their class that they were both in love with and who could play the piano.

In unison they said, "Hey, Alice."

Alice said, "Hey, Cloyce and Joyce."

Together they said, "Did Mama come home yet?"

Alice said, "No, honey."

Alice gave Cloyce and Joyce sharp knives and they chopped up celery and onions.

Douglas came in, too. He was six and always wanted to cook. Alice tied a cup towel around his waist for an apron and let him crack an egg for the biscuit dough. Douglas said, "Hey, parrot."

Dora Ethel came in, finally. She was a senior in high school. She made good grades and wore makeup. She took one look at the parrot and said, "Re-pul-seevo!" and went back in the house somewhere to do her nails. Sometimes when Dora Ethel came in and looked at the parrot she said,

"Caramba!" or "Basta!" or sometimes "Out, out, damn spot!" It all depended on her mood.

Runt was reading the newspaper. In the dim winter light he looked almost like Dr. Dust, not like the town drunk.

He was wearing eyeglasses that he had bought for a dollar out of a bin at the Arrow Drug Store. He was reading the obituaries, it was the only part of the paper he ever bothered to look at.

Alice said, "Uncle Runt, do you reckon I could talk to you for a minute?"

Runt looked up.

He said, "First thing I do, see, is run through the column"—which Runt pronounced *col-yewm*—"and check all their ages, nothing else, not even the names."

Runt was talking about the names in the obituaries.

Alice said, "Something happened today, I don't know what to make of it."

Alice imagined that this was the way that wives and husbands talked after supper. She thought this was the way she would have confided in Dr. Dust, if they were married, if something had scared her.

Runt said, "Like tonight, for example. Seventy-one, eighty-seven, sixty-three—it sounds a little bit like football, don't it?"

Alice said, "Well, it does sound like football, a little bit."

Runt said, "Here's another seventy-one, see, it's like

a pattern might be developing. I watch out for things like that."

She said, "I never thought about there being a certain technique to reading the obituaries."

Runt said, "Now here's a seventy-nine, and here's a seventy-four. Lots of seventies tonight. It's looking pretty good."

Alice said, "I took my class to visit a sick child today—"

"They're tricky, an obituary," Runt told Alice. "It's not as easy as it looks, reading one, if you do it right."

Alice said, "Uncle Runt, have you got a minute to talk to me?"

Runt looked up from his newspaper, over the top of his glasses.

Runt said, "It ain't too long, I hope, is it, peaches, I got me a business appointment I don't want to miss."

Alice knew that her uncle was not through drinking for the night, and then there was this whole obituaries business that had to be attended to.

She said, "After school, when I was walking home, I thought I saw a child. In a raindrop."

Runt said, "Well, I guess I don't know nothing about a child in a raindrop."

She said, "You're going to be seeing this one in the obituaries. The one in the raindrop was dead."

Runt looked at Alice as if he might be seeing her for the first time. Runt's face looked like, Did you say dead?

He said, "What child was this you say you seen?"

She said, "I'm not sure. Maybe the Gregg child, the one that got burned. But the child in the raindrop was dead in a river, somewhere, seemed like he got drowned."

He said, "A dead child in a river?"

She said, "Seemed like he was."

He said, "Solon Gregg's child?"

She said, "I don't know. Maybe."

Runt put the newspaper aside.

She said, "I was walking home from school today, Uncle Runt, and just when I passed by Lord and Lady Montberclair's Mexican mansion, I happened to look into a raindrop and saw this dead child in a river."

Real slow, Runt folded the newspaper. He laid it on the table beside his chair.

He said, "In a river."

Alice said, "Yessir."

Runt got up from his chair and went to the parrot's cage. He opened the big wire door on the front. He put his hand in the cage and jiggled the little bar where the big bird was sitting. The parrot stepped up off the bar and onto the back of Runt's hand, with its strong claws holding tight.

The bird was heavy. Runt put it on his shoulder. It spread

out the long red feathers of its tail, down Runt's back like a cape. The topnotch stood up like a question mark over its head.

Alice said, "Uncle Runt?"

Runt decided he would call Fortunata, his wife. He would beg her to come back, though he did not expect her to do so. It didn't take a magic raindrop to see that sad scrap of the future. Fortunata was allergic to the parrot. Maybe if he promised to get rid of it, find it a good home, she might be enticed to come back home. Runt doubted it, but he could try.

Runt said, "I ain't partial to fortune telling."

Alice said, "It's more like a dream, I think. I think I've got this boy on my mind, this Glenn, and so I thought about him in water, instead of fire. Like a regular dream."

Runt said, "These Delta rivers are full of niggers, honey."

Alice said, "Colored people?"

Runt felt sorry for Fortunata, getting mixed up with a drunken gravedigger. Long time ago Fortunata had a chance to move to Illinois, get away altogether, but she stayed with him. He wished he could have spared her falling in love with him.

Their last fight was typical, awful.

"You never—"

"You always—"

"You drunk—"

"You bitch—"

"You impotent pig—"

"You stupid whore—"

"You're drinking yourself to death, and you blame me."

For Fortunata it was one fight too many.

At the end of the fight, Fortunata said, "You're not a bad man, Runt, you truly ain't. It's God and nature that's so damn bad."

He would call her, he reckoned. Maybe he'd tell her don't come home, he was still digging his own grave with a whiskey bottle.

The parrot was warm on Runt's shoulder.

The rain was still falling outside the window.

Runt said, "Alice, honey, a child in a raindrop ain't a dream."

The parrot stood up straight and stretched itself and spread out its wings and beat them against the air and against Runt's head and face. Runt did not move, and the parrot settled down again.

Runt carried the parrot with him to the cage and put it inside and closed the wire door. He said, "I got to make that appointment I told you about."

Sometimes a little taste to settle your insides on a rainy Delta evening was the best you could do. Sometimes that was all that was left for a man to do.

Alice said, "Well, all right, then."

Runt said, "All right, then."

When her uncle was gone, Alice went to the parrot's cage. She put her face to the bars of the cage. She said, "I love you, I love you, I love you."

THE RAIN kept on falling, falling, falling, down onto Esequeena Street. The light in the barber shop was the only light on the street, except for the buzzard roosts, so late at night. The barber pole didn't turn, it was only a wooden pole. It shed the rain, that's about all.

There was nobody in the shop for a haircut this time of night, just Rage Gage, the barber, and a few friends, blues singers.

The light from the front window was yellow, and although it broke up a corner of the darkness and the rain with its small strength, it seemed to turn to water and to run and fade like cheap dye, once it left the window.

The house was not a real barber shop, not originally, though it had been fixed up nice. It was only a Negro cabin with a barber pole out in front of it.

Esequeena Street was lined with buzzards. Rage Gage didn't like cutting hair up underneath no bunch of buzzards. Especially buzzards named after white men. He wondered why the scientists down in Jackson couldn't be naming a few buzzards after colored people.

Ain't like they don't have plenty of buzzards to go

around. Half them buzzards ain't even got a name. That's the truth.

Rage Gage was sitting up in his own barber chair, feet propped up on the big steel footrest, talking with the boys about what happened down to Mr. Red's.

The barber chair was a good one, too—big, sturdy porcelain rascal, with a handle to pump the seat up and down and another handle to let the back down for a shave. Rage Gage needed a good adjustable chair, like this. One of his legs was shorter than the other, and so he had to wear a built-up rocking shoe on his right foot, and he wasn't very tall to begin with. It was a good chair for Rage, pump it right down to size.

Comfortable for the customer, too, steady as a stone. Bolted right in the floor, easy as pie, strop come with it, fastened to the armrest, good strop too, double leather, high quality Eye-talian cowhide, crack like a whip when you put a razor to it.

Rage Gage bought this chair long time ago down at Swami Don's Elegant Junk, fifteen dollars, cash money, that's what it cost, lot of jack, Jack, but twice as nice at half the price, go easy, Greasy, you got a long way to slide.

The chair had a real leather seat cushion built right in, ox-blood in color, faded, well sure, used like this, it's gone be faded some, good and broke in, that's why it's faded, so that was okay, wont even cracked, good chair, fine chair, fifteen dollars cash, that's all, a bargain, a steal, well sure it's expensive, ain't nobody said it was cheap, but worth it, sho, worth every red cent.

Used to have it over on Fourth Street, whole shop, chair and everything, combs, clippers, scissors, pomade trays, straight razors, straightening irons, shaving mugs, shaving brushes, bay rum, clothes brush, shampoo, dandruff treatment, louse dip, hot rocks to rub old men's froze-up balls with, fully equipped barber services, next! who's next! step right up, ain't nothing to be skeered of, I hope you ain't wanting one them new do's we be seeing in *Ebony*, get yo throat cut wearing one them do's in Arrow Catcher, let me slop on some of this here White Rose, give you that shiny petroleum-jelly look they's talking so much about in Paris, France, plaster that nappy got-damn rag of yore's down on yo field-nigger Ubangi-ass haid.

Somebody said, "That Chicago boy got off lucky, what I say."

Somebody else said, "Uh-huh."

The one-handed monkey was there, as usual, sitting in one of the empty theater seats, with the stuffing coming out of the seat bottoms. The monkey was holding last Sunday's funny paper up in front of his face like he was reading it. The monkey was real old and had gray hair on his head and face and armpits. It had learned a long time ago to balance one edge of a folded newspaper on its little stump of a hand and to hold the other edge with the good hand. He didn't act like no handicapped monkey.

Blue John Jackson was there, the blues man, from out in the country. He was tall and a little stooped and had a gravelly voice. He had quit drinking whiskey and smoking cigarettes a long time ago, but his voice still sounded like a whiskey drinker. About all he ever drank now was a whole heap of strong coffee, with a little sweetmilk.

Blue John brought his guitar over to the barber shop most every night since Rage Gage moved his business from Fourth Street. Blue John played "The Spoonful" sometimes, and "Little Bo Peep" and "Corrina, Corrina," if you axed him just right.

Just then the little redheaded peckerwood Roy Dale Conroy, the gravedigger's child, come easing in, white boy with a strange way about him, done snuck out of his daddy's house again, in the middle of the night.

Roy Dale said, "Hey, Rage Gage."

Rage Gage said, "Hey, Peckerwood."

Roy Dale had a timid little voice.

He said, "Y'all blowing?"

Rage Gage said, "Git one them dry towels off the sink rack."

Roy Dale took a couple of thin-cloth shaving towels off a

rack on the double sink in the middle of the floor and dried off his face and hair. Then he rubbed his neck and arms good, too.

Blue John said to Roy Dale, "She'll come back. She'll come back some day."

Roy Dale said, "I don't know."

Blue John said, "She will."

Roy Dale eased into the empty theater seat next to the one-handed monkey. The monkey looked up and saw Roy Dale and recognized him and put the newspaper aside and crawled over the chair arm and into his lap and wrapped his tail around in a circle and cuddled up close to Roy Dale's chest.

Roy Dale took off first one shoe and then the other, and then he took off his stretched-out argyle socks, and laid them out on top of the cold space heater to dry out a little.

Roy Dale was missing his mama, that was true enough.

Roy Dale said, "I heard about what happened, down at Mr. Red's."

Rage Gage said, "Where'd you hear about that?"

Roy Dale said, "Schoolyard."

Rage Gage said, "Ain't no telling how news be traveling."

Roy Dale said, "I own know."

Rage Gage said, "Well—"

There were two other people in the room. One was The

Rider, the frail, frail little albino blues man, with white nappy hair and pink skin. His eyes were always covered up with dark glasses, like blind people wear. He walked into walls. He played a Gibson guitar, which he didn't need to see. Blue John Jackson claimed he couldn't play a lick of the blues without The Rider alongside him, he took him everywhere he went.

The other person in the barber shop was the old shoe-shine boy from Red's Goodlookin Bar and Gro., Rufus McKay, who slept all day and woke up singing songs from a former time.

Rufus McKay said to Rage Gage, "How come you be letting white trash set around in your house?"

Rage said to Roy Dale, "Jefferson Davis been missing you, Face."

Sometimes he called Roy Dale Peckerwood, sometimes he called him Face. Jefferson Davis was the name of the monkey.

Roy Dale was a little scared of Rufus McKay. Rufus was tall and skinny and mean. Roy Dale didn't look up, he just petted the little monkey sitting on his lap.

Rufus McKay said, "You so worried about buzzards ain't be named Diphtheria Jean Johnson and Bessie Smith, and you go name your own monkey after a white man. And then let him sit in the lap of a piece of white trash. Give that monkey cooties."

Roy Dale said, "Fuck you, Rufus."

Rufus said, "I got a razor in my shoe, you little pecker-wood motherfucker, I'll cut your little white-trash, cracker-ass throat."

Roy Dale said, "You and whose monkey?"

The Rider, behind his dark glasses, laughed that good old albino blues-man laugh, heh, heh, heh, and never changed his expression. He strummed on his guitar, thrum, thrum, thrum. His white eyebrows showed above the top of his shades.

Blue John Jackson started tuning his guitar, *poing poing poing*, one string at a time.

Rage Gage said, "Hand me my box, Face, out the corner."

Roy Dale got up from the old theater seat, which sprung up behind him, and carried the monkey over to Rage Gage's guitar and gave the guitar to Rage and went and sat back down with Jefferson Davis again.

Blue John had his box pretty well tuned by now. He was strumming the top end, sounded like a bell ringing.

Rufus McKay said, "See how this piece of trash talk to me? What if that little Chicago nigger be talking trash like that?"

Rage Gage was in tune now, too. He started to sing a song he had written about getting evicted from his barber shop on Fourth Street.

Blue John Jackson was playing a melody, soft and complex and beautiful, above the simple words, while The Rider was playing an eight-note backbeat, boogie-woogie. The Rider learned to play backup in New Orleans, and so he thought a song wasn't no song without a backbeat.

Rufus McKay said, "Black chile talk to a white man like this little piece of trash be talking to me, I hate to think what be done happen."

Rage Gage sang about the shop on Fourth Street, a place he called his own.

Jefferson Davis loved tunes, the monkey. He turned around in Roy Dale's lap and sat facing the guitars. Roy Dale had to push his tail down out of his face so he could blow on the harp that Blue John handed him.

Blue John was running a few quiet riffs, and The Rider was backing him up.

Rufus McKay said, "Like this mawning. Little Chicago nigger be lucky he don't get throwed in the river."

Roy Dale said, "My Cousin Alice seen it in a raindrop."

Nobody said anything. Roy Dale went back to petting the monkey. He put Blue John's harmonica aside.

Rage Gage was singing about being evicted from his old barber shop and having to move into the Belgian Congo in the shadow of a flock of buzzards.

The Rider looked at Rufus McKay and nodded agreement, though he didn't stop playing the guitar. His left hand kept moving steadily up and down the neck of the guitar, his fingers lightly touching the frets to make the changes.

Blue John Jackson kept on playing his more intricate part, and he looked up at Rufus McKay as well.

Rage Gage sang around the rain and the buzzards and Vardaman and Bilbo and Ross Barnett and the scientists down in Jackson. Somehow, in this song, they were all to blame for Rage's being evicted from his shop on Fourth Street.

There was another break, and more guitars.

Rufus McKay said, "Anything happen to that boy, it's on the head of the white trash. Gravedigger be standing right on the scene, just smacking his lips, he got him some work now, look like."

Everybody knew he was talking about Roy Dale's daddy.

The music kept on. Rage Gage didn't sing a whole verse, just a line or two thrown in now and then. *Oh trouble, trouble, trouble.* Then more guitars.

Blue John Jackson said, "What'd you do about it, Rufus?" He looked back down at his strings, to help him through the riff.

The Rider leaned over close to Blue John and seemed to whisper something, though no one else could hear it.

Rufus McKay said, "Ain't nothing to do."

Blue John said, "Peckerwood's daddy walked down in the Belgian Congo, looking for him, couldn't find him."

Rage Gage sang that he always knew he wasn't going to get treated fair.

Blue John Jackson said, "White-trash gravedigger went looking for him. What'd you do, Rufus? Act like you's asleep and singing show tunes?"

The Rider laughed, heh heh heh.

Roy Dale said, "Lady Montberclair took him home in her car." This was schoolyard gossip, too. Roy Dale hoped it was true.

Blue John said, "White lady took him home."

Rufus said, "I ain't did nothing, I ain't saying I did. Wasn't none of me told him to be flirting with a white lady. Little nigger better be wolf-whistling his own kind."

They were coming to the end, the big finish, the guitars were strong.

Rufus said, "What I ain't did is kill nobody. I ain't kill no white boy for telling me to go fuck myself. That's the difference between a white man and a nigger. I jess talk. That's all I ever do, don't hurt nobody."

Rage Gage sang, *But if you come to three-seventeen Esequeena Street—*"

Blue John said, "Ain't saved no lives, neither."

Rage Gage sang, *I'll cut the buzzards out yo hair.*

Blue John said, "All right, uh-huh." And the song was over.

For a long time nobody said anything. The rain kept on falling.

Blue John put his guitar back in the case and put it aside.

Roy Dale took the monkey with him and set Rage Gage's box back in the corner of the barber shop for him and then sat back down again. The Rider held onto his guitar, across his lap.

Rage Gage said, "The buzzards is gone, leastways. Done flew back out to the swamp."

Roy Dale said, "How come Jefferson Davis has just got one hand?"

Rage Gage said, "That monkey got named long time ago, Rufus."

He was answering an earlier question.

"That's a *old* monkey. My daddy named that monkey."

Rufus said, "Wouldn't be no better to name a monkey after a nigger, no-way." Rufus was philosophical. He said, "Less he be named Rage Gage. That monkey kindly favor you."

The Rider said, Heh heh heh. His pink skin looked pinker than ever.

Rufus said, "You know what make me mad every time I think about it?—name of this town, Arrow Catcher. That's a white-man name if I ever did hear one."

Roy Dale said, "I'm going out for the arrow-catching team at school. Coach give me a bow and arrow to use."

Rufus said, "See there? Ain't no arrow-catching team out at the college in Itta Bena, out at M.V.C. Basketball, football, but ain't no arrow-catching, not one. Where's the colored arrow-catching team? Then coloreds got to live in a town name of Arrow Catcher. See what I'm saying? It ain't right."

Roy Dale said, "I shoot arrows right into the wall of my room and pretend like it's my mama and daddy."

Rage Gage said, "Somebody be done made a mojo out of Jefferson Davis's hand."

Rufus McKay said, "What somebody ought to do is get them a mojo and give it to that little Bobo boy. He gone need all the magic he can get."

Blue John Jackson said, "You know what?"

Blue John didn't talk much. People looked in his direction. The Rider stared down into the center hole in his guitar.

Blue John said, "Arrow Catcher don't be so bad for a name. You know what'd be bad? What'd be bad was if they name this here town Spear Chunker. Now that'd be bad. That's what I'd call bad."

For a long time nobody said anything. They just all looked at him.

Blue John said, "Then you could sign up for the high

school spear-chunking team, Rufus. Wouldn't need to be on no arrow-catching team."

The Rider said, Heh heh heh.

Rufus McKay said, "You make a joke like that and you jess part of the problem, Blue John. You part of the reason that child done put his life in danger, make a joke like that. You, too, Rider, laughing at it, like you some kind of mystery on the mountain. You ain't no mystery. All y'all just guilty as sin, guilty as the gravedigger, guilty as me."

5

THE ARROW Hotel was not a hotel at all, but a great big, wood-frame, two-story boarding house, with feather pillows on the beds that smelled like Vitalis and Wildroot, no meals, room and bath, two dollars a night. There was not even a desk clerk to let you in—old Miss Peabody who owned the place had stopped coming altogether, and so you just went in, left your two dollars under a shot glass near the register-book, and found yourself a place to flop.

Across the street was a place that used to be a frozen meat locker, and then it turned into a chicken sexing plant, which attracted a lot of Japanese people to town, for some reason, and now it was mostly just an empty building, except when they could rent it out to the Pentecostals for revival meetings, who played "Easter Parade" for the benediction one time, if you can believe such a thing.

On the second floor of the Arrow, in a room seldom used, Solon Gregg was lying on the bed thinking he better kill somebody tonight. He couldn't think of no way else to keep from thinking about his boy that got burned up on account of him and was laying back home in an iron bed surrounded by Get Well cards. Kill *himself*, is what he had in mind.

Nobody else was staying in the Arrow Hotel tonight,

103

not hardly, anyway. Solon signed in the big book, "John Smith," and left two one dollar bills under the shot glass on a low table next to the lamp.

Solon hoped his sister Juanita didn't have to sleep in a dump like this, or like the one he just left in New Orleans. He fingered the trigger of the little gun. He wondered how many shots he could get off into his own head, or his heart, say, before he dropped the pistol. He didn't think one shot would do the trick, even in the head, his gun was so light. Pretty soon Solon would be just like the dead man he helped pull out of the bed in New Orleans, if things went the way Solon was planning.

Solon was naked, he couldn't stand them wet clothes no longer. He took them off the minute he come in the door and slung them up in a corner. He wished he could take off his whole skin and hair. He wished the gas fire had burned all his skin off instead of his boy's. He wished he was the one laying up in an iron bed instead of his baby, that's what he wished.

The Arrow Hotel was best known as being a place to commit suicide. It had a pretty good reputation in the past, lot of people successfully died here. In the good old days you could end your sorry life in the Arrow Hotel and Miss Peabody or the housemaid would find you first thing next morning, when she's making up the bed. Or somebody would miss you at breakfast.

Well, them was the days. Now you could lay up in the Arrow for two weeks and rot before anybody found you, slow as business was since they stopped serving meals.

He was laying stretched out on the bed in a quarter inch of dust, didn't bother to turn back the covers. There was a street light outside his window, and so the room was not completely dark, there was yellow light and shadows, filtered through rain.

There was an empty chifferobe, that's about all the furniture there was. Enormous trees stood all around the hotel, ancient, really, and the rain falling through them was like whispers. Solon didn't know what the whispers were saying to him. *Kill somebody, you'll feel better.* Something like that.

Up on his bare stomach Solon had rested the pistol, the little .25 caliber revolver with the wooden handle-grips. He had took it out of his pants pocket when he slung his pants up in the corner to dry.

Just .25 caliber—it was most too light to kill anybody with, probably, less you hit them just right, vital organ, and then you couldn't really be sure, it was a crapshoot.

He put the pistol barrel in his mouth and pulled back the hammer with his thumb, until it cocked into place. He was surprised and pleased to find that the gun barrel tasted like oil.

Gun oil, well, sir, sweet as peaches. Just before he left New Orleans, he had wiped the gun off with an oily rag and so most of the oil was still there, right where he left it, doing its job of preventing undue corrosion, in spite of this wet weather we been having. This fact just seemed extra nice to Solon, warmed up his sad heart a little bit.

The thing was, though, there was something he might could do to be helpful. He took the gun barrel out of his mouth.

What he could do was get dressed again and slip back over to his own house and go back around to his boy's window, Glenn, scope him out a little, you know, up under that light bulb his mama kept burning day and night, and shoot the child in his bed. Put him out of his misery, so to speak.

Seem like the least a daddy could do, after he caused so much trouble to the tyke. It'd be the one act of kindness Solon was ever responsible for. It gave Solon a good feeling to be thinking of others for a change. It made a difference in the way he thought about himself, too. It increased his self-esteem, which had done reached a low ebb lately, to be perfectly honest.

Plus, it'd be a nice way to go out, for him as well as Glenn. In a family setting, so to speak. And that's what he would do, of course, put the lights out on himself right afterwards.

He wished he had a heavier pistol. That was the one

drawback, this durn puny little pistol. If he had him a .38 pistol, why, hell, boy, it wouldn't be no question at all. He'd pretty much be obligated to do it, if he had a .38. If he had a .38, or even a .32, really, he'd feel completely at ease in sticking his arm into the bedroom window, snapping off a couple of quick shots at his boy and then asking Glenn's mama did she and the rest of the children want they lights put out, too, just make it a family affair, the more the merrier, seem like. Last himself, of course.

Well, wait, now, let's see, hold on, he better think about this. This durn thing don't hold but six bullets. He didn't have no extras, six was all he had left, all the excitement of coming back to Mississippi, he didn't think about picking up an extra box of hollow-points.

Shit. Now ain't that the limit. Goddamn, if it wont one dang thing, it's another. Well, okay, let's see, how many children did he have, anyway, counting Wanda. And Glenn. Four, wasn't it? Plus hisself and his wife, that's six.

Actually, that was perfect, if he didn't have to shoot anybody twice. Well, but, anyway, Wanda might want to just pass on her turn, see, with her getting married and all. Wanda might want to go on down to Missouri to the ranch, so, you know, Solon could shoot somebody twice, if necessary. That possibility certainly had to be taken into consideration. He'd just wait and ask Wanda, that was the thing to do, now that he thought about it. Better safe than sorry, like the poet said. Solon didn't want to act impulsively, spoil the whole surprise.

Solon's pile of rain-drenched clothes was flopped over there in the corner of the room like wet roadkill. It looked like a big, cold carcass of a hellhound that's done shucked off its mortal coil with the help of a Kenworth hauling pulpwood out on Highway 61 to Memphis.

He didn't want to put back on some wet clothes, now that he was settled in. Comfort meant a lot to a man about to kill himself, even if others had to want.

He began to feel a little chilly, just thinking about putting those wet clothes back on. He fingered the trigger of the pistol and placed the barrel against his teeth and tongue again, tasting the sweet oil. This had been one long, hard day, have mercy, he felt like he deserved him a long rest.

He took the pistol barrel out of his mouth and thought about going in the bathroom down the hall and seeing did the tank have any hot water in it, he might like to take hisself a good steamy tub bath. Warm his bones, although right now he believed he'd try not to think about his bones.

Instead, he got up off the bed and turned the covers back and slid in between the sheets, oh Law, they felt good upon his nekkidness, yes they did.

He pulled the covers back up to his chin and felt the

warmth close around him. It seemed pretty durn lonely to die all by yourself in the Arrow Hotel. He looked at the pile of clothes. He might put them back on, go out one more time tonight.

He thought about New Orleans. Was it only yesterday, last night, he'd taken his earnings from the robberies and bought hisself a bus ticket and slept so sound to the music of the wheels, trucking on down on the road? He thought about himself asleep on that Greyhound, and the thought of it was so sweet it almost made him cry.

It was like he was outside of himself, watching Solon Gregg fall asleep in his seat. Looking at himself there, up by the tinted-glass window of that old Greyhound cruiser, it didn't seem possible that he was who he was, the robber and killer and wife beater. Confession makes the heart grow fonder, as his crazy wife used to say.

Who he really looked like to himself, sleeping there in that bus, was Bo Peep, the one in the song. Like he was Bo Peep. *She came trucking, back on down the line.*

It scared him to think that murder and suicide might be just another vain dream, an ideal hope that, once it was accomplished, would turn out to be just like New Orleans, just like everything else in this life, nowhere near what it was cracked up to be, and only another way of feeling bad about himself.

He had the pistol under the cover with him, in his

hand, and he dreamed that he had killed everybody, his whole family and himself. Glenn, of course, laying dead and smiling in his bloody sheets. Killing him had healed his burns and taken away his scars. He was the same beautiful child he once was, with a Roy Rogers school satchel and a milk jug full of gasoline.

Even Wanda, too, and her new husband, who had said they didn't want to be left out. They were there, dead and covered with blood. Even Juanita and her pimp husband, and their sweet little nigger baby, covered with blood, hair all over the walls, legs and arms crisscrossed everywhere on the linoleum floor of the Gregg's house.

It was a happy dream, and filled with hope, although Solon wondered where he had come up with so many bullets. He must have won the bullet lottery. And he must have gotten holt of a heavier pistol too, .38 caliber at least, Solon would have to guess, judging by the amount of carnage.

Well, so that was a load off his mind. Everybody was cold, stone dead. In the dream Solon was dead, too, of course, but he could still see the whole scene and know that he had done the right thing.

So it surprised him that when he woke up, found out he was not only not dead but that he seemed to have been having a completely different dream from the one he thought he was having, and this one, the one in his waking head, was not even about himself and his family. He seemed to be having a dream about the Montberclairs.

They were in the Mexican house. Solon saw the great trees, the birdbaths and fountains and pools, the sun porches and Mexican furniture and framed pictures of horses, the pure white rooms and glass tables.

Sally Anne Montberclair seemed to have fixed up a little room of her own, a former utility room, off the main carport. Had it been only this morning that Solon visited in this home? It seemed so long ago.

Sally Anne's narrow little bed was arranged neatly along one wall of the room, and the bed was made up with an Indian blanket of some kind, with geometric designs woven in, in bright colors. The blanket was turned back in a casual way to reveal a triangle of the taut, white sheet. At the head of the bed lay two fat, clean pillows with white pillowcases.

A portable typewriter with a clean page of typing paper sat on a low table. A small, simple, red-painted ladder-back chair that Sally Anne had bought for herself in Mexico was pulled up to the typewriter table, and that was where Sally Anne was now sitting. There were a few other things that you could tell belonged only to her as well, including a handmade basket with a book in it that Solon somehow knew to be her diary.

Poindexter Montberclair had read the diary. That's what

this scene was all about. He picked up the diary and accused her with it, a book bound in red leather, and then he flung it back into the basket.

She said, "I should have told you. I was going to tell you."

Sally Anne Montberclair looked really scared.

He said, "You were going to tell me. Oh, well, that's fine, that's just fine, that makes it all right, then, doesn't it? When were you going to tell me?"

She said, "I don't know. I've been praying about it. I was trying to choose a good time to tell you."

He said, "You've been praying about it. That's rich, Sally Anne, that's really rich."

What the diary told Poindexter was that Sally Anne had slept with another man. It just came right out and said it, described it, in fact, you didn't have to read between the lines.

A younger man at that, ten years younger than Sally Anne, a kid. He played the organ on Sundays in the Episcopal church, St. George by the Lake. In her diary, Sally Anne compared the two of them, this kid and her husband, and said that sex with this other man was like a whole different experience, that nothing could ever be so good. She went on and on about fucking this boy. She said she had never felt so filled up with goodness, it was an aesthetic experience, time stood still, it was spiritual, goddamn.

Poindexter carried the Luger in the front of his pants, as usual.

She said, "Poindexter, I do want to talk about this, if you want to. You deserve that much, and more. But please, you'll have to put the gun away, won't you? Please put the gun in your drawer until we finish talking. You're scaring me."

Poindexter said, "How many times, bitch?"

She said, "That's not fair. It just isn't. You can't expect me to answer questions like that."

What really galled the living shit out of Poindexter Montberclair was that the boy who was fucking his wife was a known homosexual. Biggest goddamn queer Arrow Catcher, Mississippi, ever produced, and it had produced a few. In a town the size of Arrow Catcher, not much escaped the notice of its citizens.

The boy's name was Hoyty-Toyty McCarty, that's what they called him, Poindexter didn't know his real name, puny little cocksucker with pale skin and pale hair and known to have a dick like a goddamn Mexican donkey. Just nobody knew he was using it on married women. Or maybe everybody did. Maybe everybody in Arrow Catcher knew except Poindexter.

He said, "How many times?"

She said, "A few. I don't know. Not many."

He said, "How many?"

Sally Anne was trembling, she was scared not to answer.

She said, "Do you mean, how many different *occasions*, or how many times on each occasion?"

Poindexter said, "Jesus Christ!"

She said, "Really, Dexter, that gun makes me nervous."

He said, *"Occasions!* Oh, Jesus, Sally Anne, how could you do this to me!"

He took the gun out of his pants and pointed it at her. One time in Korea when he was a cavalry scout, second lieutenant, he sprayed automatic-rifle fire into some dense brush around a stand of baobab trees outside of a jungle village called Sing Tu and killed eight people before he even saw anything move. That was the drill, that was the way it was done, preventative action, shoot first, ask questions later.

After he stopped shooting, he heard some groaning, so he opened up again until the groaning stopped. He told a sergeant and a couple of younger boys to drag them out by their feet. Now, right now!

Half of the dead were men in uniforms, half of them, he didn't know, kids, old folks. Any one of them could have killed him. He remembered that his rifle barrel was hot as a firecracker, you could light a cigarette on it.

The other soldiers looked at Lieutenant Montberclair with something like awe.

The sergeant said, "Jesus, Lieutenant, I didn't see a thing."

They thought he had known what he was doing.

Lieutenant Montberclair held the rifle barrel up to his lips and blew the smoke away, or pretended to, and when he did, his breath across the barrel made a little whistling sound, wheeee. He flashed them his big, bright southern smile.

He said, "Sharp eye, sergeant, sharp eye," and winked. He said this in his southern way, "Shop eye, sah-junt, shop eye," for increased effect.

In Sally Anne's little room, he held the pistol against Sally Anne's forehead until it made a little red ring on the skin between her eyes. He said, "How many more were there? I don't mind killing you, I don't mind killing you in the least, so let's just have a few answers, all right, Sally Anne? How many more did you fuck?"

She said, "Dexter, honey, please, don't do this."

He said, "Open your mouth, Sally Anne, like you opened it for all those men's cocks."

He slipped the pistol barrel between her teeth.

Solon Gregg didn't know how Lord Montberclair had found him here in the Arrow Hotel. Maybe he went by Solon's house and found out from his wife. Maybe the Arrow Hotel was only the obvious place for a person at the end of the line, like Solon, to wind up.

Anyway, when he finally started to come to a little bit,
out of this heavy sleep, he realized that Lord Montberclair must have been standing in the room talking to him
for some time. The story Lord Montberclair was telling
him, about Sally Anne's adulteries, had gotten mixed up
into Solon's dreams. He wondered what he had missed,
which parts he had added. He wondered if it was true
that the Episcopal organist was really a queer, Hoyty-Toyty
McCarty. He heard it often enough, but you never can tell,
you don't want to jump to conclusions about people and
their preferences. People are all time claiming somebody's
queer and they ain't. Still, Solon had always admired the
way that young man looked, and talented, too.

At first Solon thought Lord Montberclair was asking him
to murder Hoyty-Toyty McCarty for him, the organist.
That was the distinct impression Solon was receiving about
the gist of this whole conversation, though he was willing
to admit he might have missed a few of the subtler points.

But no, he wont, that wont it at all. Lord Montberclair was asking Solon to murder the little nigger, the
sassy-mouth boy in Red's Goodlookin Bar and Gro. this
morning, Bobo. Now wasn't that something? Make a mistake like that. Solon figured he better listen up a little bit,
try to get caught up on this here conversation before he
commenced to offering any strong opinions of his own.

Lord Montberclair was drunk. Even Solon could smell

him, halfway across the room. Brandy, and a lot of it. He must have been drunk, too, when he was pointing that Luger at his wife.

Solon himself had started to sober up a little bit, and his stomach was feeling a little queasy. And a familiar feeling was coming back to him.

He was feeling like if he didn't do something soon, kill somebody, something, almost anything, to make meaning out of all this pain of his, and his baby boy laying up in a bed looking like an Egyptian mummy, well, he just didn't know what would happen to him, he didn't know how he was going to endure one more minute on this awful planet Earth.

Poindexter said, "You said he bragged about fucking a white woman, didn't you, isn't that what you said."

Solon said, "That's right."

Poindexter said, "You said he had a white woman's picture in his wallet, didn't you, isn't that right?"

Solon said, "That's right."

Poindexter said, "He made lewd remarks to Sally Anne, and they drove off together in my car."

Solon said, "That's right."

Poindexter said, "Wolf-whistled at her."

Solon said, "That's right."

Poindexter said, "I need a man like you, Solon."

Solon said, "You do?"

Poindexter said, "Decent whitefolks have always needed the likes of you."

Solon said, "They have?"

Poindexter said, "We need people like you to help keep our niggers in line."

Solon said, "Well—"

Poindexter said, "That's how I see it, Solon, don't you agree? Isn't that how you see it?"

Solon said, "Well—"

Poindexter said, "It gives you lower classes, you white-trash boys, some *raison d'être*, wouldn't you say so?"

Solon said, "Pretty much, yeah, I guess so."

Poindexter said, "You know what pisses me off the most, though? You know what makes me want that little son-of-a-bitch hurt, really bad hurt?"

Solon said, "What's that?"

Poindexter said, "It's him carrying that white girl's picture around in his pocket. I got to thinking about that."

Solon said, "Uh-huh."

Poindexter said, "I got to thinking about that picture in his wallet. What's a nigger doing with a wallet anyway, you know?"

Solon said, "Well—"

Poindexter said, "You don't have a wallet do you, Solon? You yourself probably don't have a wallet, am I right?"

Solon said, "I been meaning to get one."

Poindexter said, "So you see? Do you see the arrogance involved here? He's got a wallet, in the first place, and now we find out about the picture?"

Solon said, "Uh-huh."

Poindexter said, "The point is, though, the picture, see? That's worse than fucking her, carrying her picture around in his pocket—wouldn't you agree?"

Solon said, "I guess it is, yeah."

Poindexter said, "I wouldn't want Hoyty-Toyty McCarty carrying a picture of Sally Anne around in his pocket."

Solon said, "Well—"

Poindexter said, "I'm getting off the point, though, Solon. I'm rambling a little. I had a cocktail before I came over here, to calm my nerves, do you understand that?"

Solon said, "A cocktail, you bet."

Poindexter said, "Carrying that picture around with him was as much as saying he owned that girl. Not just fucked her, Solon, owned her, like a wife."

Solon said, "Uh-huh."

Poindexter said, "That's what irks me so bad. That's what lets me know that this can't be allowed to stand unpunished."

Solon said, "And you're saying you think I'm the man for the job."

Poindexter said, "Well, yes, of course. It's the order of things, more or less."

Solon said, "It's my role in life to keep the niggers in line for you rich people."

Poindexter said, "It's not money, Solon. It's *quality*."

Solon said, "I see."

Poindexter said, "You'll do it then? Wonderful! That's fine. I knew you wouldn't let me down."

Solon said, "Okay, I'll do it. I'll take care of him for you. Pistol-whip his ass in an inch of his life."

Lord Montberclair said, "Splendid!"

Solon was making plans of his own. First thing was, he planned to ask Lord Montberclair for five hundred dollars, not a cent less.

Solon said, "You ain't heard whose pitcher that boy was carrying around in his pocket, have you?"

Poindexter said, "What do you mean?"

Solon said, "I just wondered did you know whose pitcher the nigger was toting in his wallet, is all, just a matter of curiosity, didn't mean nothing."

Poindexter said, "It was his white girlfriend, wasn't it? Isn't that what you told me? I just assumed it was his girlfriend from Chicago."

Solon said, "Well, could be, could be, I didn't get a good look at the pitcher my ownself."

Poindexter said, "Well, but who else could it be? What are you saying here, Solon?"

Solon said, "Ain't none of me saying something. Me, I'm just wondering. I'm just wondering if that pitcher in the nigger's wallet wont some local girl. Some white lady from right around town, here."

Lord Montberclair said, "I want him dead. I want to see that nigger dead."

Solon said, "Uh-huh."

Lord Montberclair said, "I'll pay you a thousand dollars."

Solon fingered the pistol beneath the sheet.

He said, "I don't know about that."

Lord Montberclair said, "What else do you want? It's all the money I can offer."

Solon said, "I ain't got no car. Cain't make no successful getaway without a getaway car."

Lord Montberclair said, "Take the bus. I'll give you a thousand dollars and a bus ticket to anywhere in the world."

Solon shook his head, real slow, side to side.

He said, "I don't thank so, my friend. Tell you the truth, I'd feel like a durn fool making my desperate escape on a Greyhound bus. Do you see what I mean? What you want me to do, Dexter, stand out in front of the Arrow Cafe with a bunch of sharecroppers and wait till ten o'clock tomorrow morning for the southbound to pull in? You want me to stand in line and let some old boy in a baggy gray wool suit and run-down shoes and a bill cap punch my ticket and check my luggage? Honest to God, Dexter, you might ought to think about getting a grip on that drinking problem of yours, if that's your solution to how to escape the scene of a murder. You ain't getting out enough. You ought to take in a movie now and then, take a trip somewhere besides Mexico."

Solon was still naked beneath the covers of the bed. He had sat up now, against his pillows, but he kept the covers pulled up high on his chest. He could see the Luger in Lord Montberclair's pants, and so he kept his hand on his own pistol, up under the covers, pointed at Lord Montberclair's stomach.

Lord Montberclair said, "If you take my car and they catch up with you, I'll be implicated."

Solon said, "Well, ain't that just tough shit, Dexter. I mean, boo-fuckin-hoo, man. Scuse me if I ain't too goddamn over-sympathetic. I ain't planning to get caught. It just ain't a part of God's universal plan for the white-trash element to keep the niggers in line for you quality people and then go to jail for you, too. And if I do get caught, well hell, man, use your imagination, tell them I stole the car, for God's sake, that's simple enough, ain't it? Who's gone believe the word of a piece of white trash like me over that of a fine gent like your ownself?"

Lord Montberclair said, "Well, that's true, that's true

enough, I hadn't thought about it that way. I'm not thinking too clearly these days, you understand, family matters, you're a family man, you understand what I mean. Nobody's going to believe a piece of shit like you."

Solon said, "If you turn me in, Dexter, I'll kill you and everybody you ever met, bank on it."

Lord Montberclair said, "Okay, all right, is that it, then? A thousand dollars and a car. That's fair, that sounds fair enough, I see your point. You can take the El Camino. I'd give you the Cadillac, but I don't know where it is. Anyway, you'll be needing transportation out to the nigger's house. I know where he lives. Sally Anne took him home, well you know that, you're the one who told me about her and the big buck in the first place. Anyhow, I know where he's staying."

Solon said, "There's one more thing."

Lord Montberclair said, "What's that?"

Solon said, "I want that Luger."

Instinctively, Lord Montberclair's hand went to the pistol in his belt.

Beneath the sheets, Solon Gregg lifted the little .25 caliber revolver and cocked the hammer with his thumb. The barrel was poking into the covers.

Lord Montberclair didn't seem to notice, and he didn't take the Luger out of his pants, he only rested his hand on it in a protective way.

Solon said, "The Luger and an extra clip. What would that be, eighteen shots altogether?"

Solon thought this was a golden opportunity. Well, just think about it. This was the first real career break he'd ever had in his life, and coming at such an opportune moment as this. It just looked like one of those cases of being in the right place at the right time. He couldn't ask for a better deal if he'd thought it up himself.

He could do this one job, snuff the nigger, then come cruising back into town in that sweet little El Camino, tool on over to his own house, and how would you say it, close down his family life forever, end on a positive note.

If Wanda didn't want to go out with the rest, and it was a distinct possibility with the upcoming wedding in the docket, why then, that was her choice and hers alone, he wouldn't try to influence her one way or the other. And here was the real kicker—he could give her the thousand dollars as a wedding present.

Goddamn, what an idea! It was positively brilliant. Whoever said "the Lord will provide" sure as shit knew what they were talking about. Why, shit, he wouldn't even have to snuff the nigger. He could pistol-whip that little motherfucker, scare the shit out of him, and then forget about him forever, just take care of family business and let Poindexter Montberclair go to hell. That nigger would just find Dr. Hightower and get hisself a couple of stitches and, it wouldn't be long, he would be eating crawfish and turnip greens while Poindexter's thousand dollars would be riding in Wanda's pocket on the first air-conditioned, double-decker Greyhound bus to Missouri, and Solon Gregg and his lovely wife and children would be managing a full-scale, high-yield indoor worm farm before that durn fool Poindexter Montberclair knew what had happened.

Some days you just have to hang in there for a while, and endure the worst that life has to offer, self-doubt and hard luck and low self-esteem, the whole shooting match, before events just seem to turn themselves around 180 percent, as Solon's wife would say, and good things start to happening, you couldn't stop them if you tried. It's just one of life's little unexplainable ironies.

That's what Solon Gregg was thinking, as Lord Poindexter Montberclair handed over the Luger and one thousand dollars cash money and the keys to the El Camino. Lord Montberclair said there was an extra clip in the glove compartment of the car, fully loaded.

In Jesus all things were possible, if you only believed—that's what the church song said, and looked like to Solon it mought be right, sho did.

And Solon and his wife might want to take their time a little, maybe go on a little vacation trip, after all the tykes were dead, so much stress and all, she deserved it, if any woman in the world did, a second honeymoon, maybe, a trip down to the Big Easy, where Solon could show her the sights, French architecture and good food, and fall in love all over again, before he used the Luger to put the lights out for both of them.

Solon said, "One more thing, Dexter."

Dexter said, "What."

Solon said, "I don't know where the place is at, where the nigger is staying. You're going with me."

6

Sims and Hill was the name of a country store a few miles outside of Arrow Catcher where you could buy beer any time of the day or night, whiskey, too, if you wanted it.

Solon was behind the wheel of the El Camino. Dexter was sitting beside him. The radio was turned to WOKJ, the colored station in Jackson. Muddy Waters was wailing away on his harmonica and going plink-plank-plunk on his guitar. Muddy Waters might be a nigger, but he spoke the truth.

Solon said this to Poindexter, "Ain't that right, Dexter?"

Dexter was feeling a little sick. He didn't answer.

Solon had his foot in the El Camino's gas tank, headed out dark, dark Highway 49 to Leflore, with empty fields, black as hell, stretching out on either side of the highway all the way to the rivers.

Dexter said, "Slow down some."

Solon didn't slow down.

Dexter said, "No need to drive all the way out on the highway to get to Runnymede, anyway. We could have crossed the bridge in Arrow Catcher."

Solon said, "Then I wouldn't get no chance to see what this little car would do."

Solon was wearing Lord Montberclair's dry clothes, too. Now that was a good one, wont it?—khaki twill pants, blue button down shirt, seersucker sport coat, a baseball cap on his head that said Leflore Country Club. Shit. Solon looked like a spote hisself.

He checked himself in the rearview mirror. Looking good. Feeling fine.

Solon said, "Drinking wine, spotey-otey, drinking wine." The song popped into his head.

Poindexter said, "Just watch where you're going. Keep your hands on the wheel."

Solon might not kill nobody after all. No need to, really. He had the car beneath him. He had the German Luger, heavy as an anvil, and the extra clip full of bulldogs, laying on the seat beside him. Plus, he had the popshooter, the .25 caliber sidearm, in his pocket, just for fun. He felt safe for the first time in his life. Oh, it was a fine night, all right, fine as wine. But not necessarily a night when anybody had to die.

It was seven or eight miles to Sims and Hill. Rain was still falling, and the clouds were low. Dark, dark Mississippi 49, a ribbon of streaming wet asphalt across the swampland. No Highway Patrol out tonight. Dock of the moon, dockside of the moon.

Solon had the El Camino rocking. Hundred and ten miles an hour. Telephone poles, flash on by!

The Runnymede flatwoods, out to the right of them, were filling up with water. Foxes and deer were camped out together on any little bit of high ground they could find.

The road beneath him was a river. Solon was moving, he was grooving, he was shucking, he was jiving, he was balling the jack.

Muddy Waters was crying on WOKJ: *I'm going down to Louisiana, baby, behind the sun.*

Poindexter said, "Have you ever heard about hydroplaning?"

Solon knew that the El Camino had risen up off the highway, that he was driving on water alone now.

Behind the sun. That's where Solon was going, that's where he already was, it was where he lived.

Hundred and fifteen miles an hour, hundred and sixteen, seventeen. Nothing but water. No contact at all with the surface of the road. Hydroplane, oh yes!

Solon said, "You gone worry yourself to an early grave, Dexter."

In this car, with these two pistols and this dry suit of college-boy clothes, Solon was filled with the power of God, not just God, the power of all the gods.

In this car at 120 miles an hour, the low clouds and dark woods around him like a cage, Solon was God. He was not Simon Peter, that chickenshit apostolic wimp of little faith who fucked around when he had a chance to stand on the flood and water ski into Glory. Solon was the Living Christ, walking on the waves.

Solon was going Christ one better, he was not walking like some goddamn peasant, he was driving on water, and driving an El Camino, to boot.

Behind the sun.

With a Luger on the seat, bulldogs in the clip, a country club baseball cap on his head.

Muddy Waters's guitar was going *pewww-boink-boink-boink, pewww-boink-boink-boink.*

Muddy Waters said, *I'm going down to New Orleans, get me a mojo hand.*

Solon Gregg was going down to New Orleans, all right, just like the voice on WOKJ, but he didn't need no mojo. He didn't need no black-cat bone, he didn't need no John the Conqueroo, nothing. Solon Gregg could walk on water. Drive on it. What did he need a mojo for, didn't make no sense, now did it?

He saw the yellow light bulb on the porch of Sims and Hill, the overhang, and the dimmer light from the gas pump, so he let up on the gas and allowed the El Camino to come back down to earth.

Poindexter said, "What are you doing?"

Solon said, "Stopping for a little taste."

Poindexter said, "Have you lost your mind?"

Solon said, "You gone say the wrong thing to me, one of these days, Dexter."

The car slowed. Solon tested the brakes, a little skid, a little slide-and-sleeve, and then tested them again, and put on his blinker and got to going slow enough so he could ease the car into the gravel drive of the country store.

Poindexter said, "You must want to get us caught. Is that what's going on here?"

Solon said, "Just think about Sally Anne sitting down on that little nigger's face, her pitcher up in his wallet like it is."

Poindexter said, "I should have killed you, is what I should have done."

Solon parked up under the overhang in the front and set the parking brake and slipped the Luger and the cartridge clip into the pocket of the seersucker jacket, for safe keeping. It paid to be a little discreet.

He said, "I meant what I said, Dexter."

Poindexter stayed in the car when Solon got out.

Solon buttoned Lord Montberclair's seersucker jacket in front to cover the pistol handle of the little revolver, where it stuck out of his belt.

He motioned for Poindexter to roll down his window. He said, "If you try to run, I'll put a bullet through your heart, Dexter. Got it?"

Poindexter didn't answer.

Solon said again, "Got it?"

Poindexter said, "Yes."

A boy name of Hydro Raney was keeping Sims and Hill open all night. Hydro was about thirty years old and had a big head. Hydro's head was as big as a goddamn watermelon. He didn't have good sense. He could run about forty miles an hour in short bursts, and he liked to chase cars. He also howled at the fire whistle, which was embarrassing to Hydro's daddy, Mr. Raney, down at the fish camp. Mr. Sims was a good man to let Hydro keep the store for him sometimes.

Solon would almost rather have had a child laying up in an iron bed with no skin or future than to have Hydro for a boy. Hydro's daddy owned a fish camp on Roebuck Lake and generally Hydro didn't do nothing all day but eat peach pie.

Just for a second there, Solon thought about pulling out the Luger and putting a bullet in that big old watermelon head, just to see what would happen. Bust that big head of Hydro's wide open. Then he thought about robbing the place and pistol-whipping the shit out of him and going on about his business.

Solon was disappointed that Hydro was keeping the store tonight. Nobody to show his money roll to. Hydro Raney didn't know the difference between a thousand dollars and a thousand and one Arabian nights.

Solon said, "Hydro, wipe that shit-eating grin off your face, or I'll shoot you square in your big ugly head."

Hydro said, "How come you dressed up like Mr. Dexter?"

Solon said, "Dexter's out in the car. We gone kill a nigger."

Hydro said, "You better not, I'll tell my daddy."

Solon said, "Gimme a beer, you watermelon-headed motherfucker. Gimme a Pearl."

Hydro said, "Pearl beer ain't no good."

Solon said, "Just gimme one, Hydro. Goddamn."

Hydro said, "Pearl beer got fish shit in it."

Solon said, "Hydro, goddamn, man!"

Hydro said, "Pearl beer is made out of water from the Pearl River, got turtle eggs in it."

Solon said, "You done spoiled my goddurn appetite, Hydro."

Hydro said, "How come you dressed up like Mr. Dexter?"

Solon said, "I ain't dressed up like nobody. Gimme a Dixie."

Hydro said, "Dixie beer ain't no good."

Solon said, "Hydro, let me tell you something, boy. Up

under this here sports jacket, right here inside my belt, I'm carrying me a pistol, see. And in my side pocket, I got another one, a big one. And so, listen here, Hydro, because it's important that you know this: if you don't give me a Dixie beer, right this here minute, without no more conversation, which I guar-awn-tee you I ain't interested in anyway, I'm going to pull out one of these here pistols and shoot you square in the head with it, now is that clear, Hydro, are you beginning to get my drift?"

Hydro said, "Is it Mr. Dexter's pistol?"

Solon said, "I give up. Calf rope."

Hydro said, "Mr. Dexter let me shoot his pistol one time."

Solon said, "He did? He let a big-headed idiot like you fire this excellent German pistol of his?"

Hydro said, "Yep."

Solon didn't know why it irritated him that Hydro Raney had fired the pistol that he had just slipped into his pocket.

He said, "Well, ain't that something. Wont that nice."

Hydro said, "I shot a gar. A three-hundred-pound gar."

Solon said, "Three hundred pounds!"

Hydro said, "Yep."

Solon said, "That's a big damn gar."

Hydro said, "I know. I shot it."

Solon said, "With the German Luger pistol?"

Hydro said, "Yep."

Solon said, "You were able to get the gar up out of the water after you shot it and weigh it?"

Hydro said, "It was already out of the water when I shot it. It was hanging on a hook at the fish camp."

Solon said, "It was hanging on a hook?"

Hydro said, "Yep."

Solon said, "You shot one of your daddy's fish, hanging out on the dock?"

Hydro said, "Yep."

Solon said, "Your daddy caught a fish that big and hung it up and you shot it with a German Luger?"

Hydro said, "Yep."

Solon said, "Seem like that was kind of dangerous, don't it?"

Hydro said, "Maybe."

Solon said, "What did your daddy say about that?"

Hydro said, "He didn't say nothing."

Solon said, "He didn't say nothing?"

Hydro said, "Nope."

Solon said, "Did he call you a fool?"

Hydro said, "Naw."

Solon said, "Did he say to go howl at the fire truck? Go chase a car? Did he call you an idiot?"

Hydro said, "Naw."

Solon said, "Did he say he was going to pistol-whip you?"

Hydro said, "Well, yeah."

Solon laughed. He said, "Okay, what else did he say?"

Hydro said, "Well—"

Solon said, "What did he say? Was it funny? Did everybody in the fish camp fall out laughing?"

Hydro said, "He said, 'I love you, my darling son, don't ever leave me, without you my life has no meaning.'"

A FEW miles away, Uncle and Auntee lay together in their bed and listened to the sad, low music of the rain on the tin roof. The sheets and pillow slips were freshly laundered and dried in the house and ironed with a slab of iron that Auntee heated on the stove.

The pillows were made of pin feathers and down from ducks raised in the yard. The bed was iron and the bedsprings creaked when either one of them moved, even a little bit. There was a clean enamel slop jar beside the bed, just in case somebody had to go during the night, and somebody always did, Uncle always.

Auntee was wearing a homemade cotton-sack nightdress. Uncle, he wasn't wearing nothing, big old nut-brown man that he was.

Auntee had wound up the clock, but now in the dark it ticked so loud she wished she could throw it out in the swamp. She thought about what Miss Sally Anne had said. Auntee thought maybe she might better call up Bobo's mama, send Bobo back home on the City of New Orleans a few days early.

The rain kept on drumming. No foxes barked tonight, no scritch owls called from the barn.

Auntee said, "He fed a right smart on that cawn-bread and sweet-tater." She was talking about Bobo, who had eaten such a big supper.

Uncle said, "He was hongry."

She said, "He drunk him some sweetmilk, too."

He said, "He was thirsty."

Then they lay together for a long time then, and didn't talk. Just the rain on the roof. Just the last spew and hiss of the little fire in the cookstove.

Auntee thought Uncle might have dropped off to sleep.

She shifted around in the bed, making the springs creak, testing whether he was sleeping. She couldn't tell.

She said, "Uncle."

After a few seconds, Uncle said, "Whut."

She said, "You ain't sleep, is you?"

He said, "I ain't sleep."

She said, "Is Bobo gone be all right?"

Now Uncle shifted in the bed, and the springs made their friendly sound, like a pine tree in winter.

She turned towards him in the bed and let Uncle hold the coarse cloth of her cotton-sack nightdress against the coarse old silk of his nakedness. Uncle smelled like sweet woodsmoke and green cane. Auntee smelled like hot lard and cornmeal.

Uncle said, "If love would save him, wouldn't no harm come to him."

In a little while they were kissing. In a little while longer, they made their slow sweet love.

The iron bed sounded like a pine forest in an ice storm, like a switch track in a Memphis trainyard, like the sweet electrical thunder of habitual love and the tragical history of the constant heart. Auntee finished first, and then Uncle soon after, and their lips were touching lightly as they did.

The rain was still falling and the scritch owl was still asleep and the dragonflies were hidden like jewels somewhere in deep brown wet grasses, nobody knew where.

Uncle rolled away from his wife and held onto her hand, never let it go, old friend, old partner, passionate wife.

Auntee pulled her nightdress back down, mostly to keep the big wet spot on the mattress from her bare butt, and then for a while they only breathed together, side by side, heavy at first, and then not so heavy, and then the comfortable breathing, like sighs, lovers before sleep.

Uncle and Auntee didn't see any car lights. Solon switched off the lights of the El Camino and rolled the last fifty yards towards the cabin, down the slick dirt road in the dark.

He said, "Is this it?"

Poindexter said, "Yes."

Rain was still falling. No radio, no Muddy Waters, only the silence of the fields.

Auntee said, "Uncle, did you hear something?"

Uncle said, "Well—"

Auntee said, "Sound like a car."

Uncle swung his feet off the side of the bed and felt around in the dark for his overalls.

Solon used a handkerchief that he found in the back pocket of Lord Montberclair's khakis to wipe fog off the inside of the windshield. The gumbo mud beneath the tires was slick as grease, and so he was worried that, in the dark, the El Camino would slide into a ditch.

It didn't, though. It held the narrow road, along the canebrake, up to the cabin beneath the cottonwood trees.

Uncle and Auntee were both dressed when they heard boots, brogans, clumping up their front steps, onto the porch.

Now Solon started to be mad again. The closer he came, the madder he got. Poindexter was right, now that he thought about it.

If Solon his ownself had to bow and scrape and call a blond-headed slut in a raincoat "Lady this" and her drunken husband "Lord that," well, why should a little nigger in a felt fedora be allowed to wolf-whistle her and call her "baby." It wont fair. Solon wondered what kind of pistol-whipping he his ownself would have took in a similar situation.

Uncle and Auntee were standing behind him wringing their hands when Solon pulled Bobo out of the bed by his feet.

Solon said, "Get out of that goddamn bed, boy, you going for a ride."

Uncle said, "Don't take him, Mr. Solon. I'd be satisfied if you just gived him a good whuppin."

Solon wasn't pointing the Luger. He still held it reversed in his hand, the way he had used it to knock on the door right before he busted in. It hung casually by the side of his leg.

Solon said, "Boy, we going for a ride. Put your pants on."

Auntee said, "Don't take him, Mr. Solon."

Solon was surprised to hear his own name spoken under this foreign roof, a second time now. He looked up at Auntee.

He said, "Did somebody tell you I was coming?"

Uncle said, "It would satisfy me if you would just whup him."

Auntee said, "Is that all you can say? Is that the onliest words you ever learned to speak in this world?—you'd be satisfied with a whupping?—that's it?"

Solon said, "Put on some pants."

He said, "Don't forget to bring the pitcher of your white girlfriend. I got somebody out in the car might want to take a look at it."

Poindexter was right about that, too. How come a nigger would be thinking he owned a white girl, carrying her pitcher around in his pocket?

Auntee said, "You ain't gone shoot him, is you?"

Solon said, "Step back."

The rain was falling, falling, falling on the tin roof of the cabin. The wind was high in the cane.

Auntee thought hard about what she was going to say next, because if it didn't work, she would hate herself for the rest of her life. She said it anyway.

She said, "Mr. Solon, would you like to set down a spell, rest your weary bones?"

Auntee's own Auntee Reena down in Balance Due was a slave-child. Auntee Reena say she don't know jess how old she is, don't keep up with it. She say she's a big girl at the Surrender, all she know. She say she chase along after the Blue soldiers' horses when they ride in. She say it's like a parade, that day, so many Blue soldiers.

That's what Auntee's Auntee Reena remember. She blind now, she bout half crazy, too, she poke a piece of bloodmeat in a fire ain't even burning, think she cook it, just ashes is all, eat right out of the cold ashes, think it be done cooked, raw as it can be, bloodmeat, too, she howl like a dog, Law.

Auntee Reena say slave she have to do all manner of things with a man you hate, slave do, jess staying alive. What Auntee got to do ain't nothing. What Auntee got to do, easy. That's what Auntee think Auntee Reena would tell her, if Auntee Reena was here right now with some good advice, if Auntee Reena had the sense God give a billygoat.

Auntee said, "Gots some frush coffee on the kitchen stove."

Auntee was just about to break bread with her grand-baby's killer. Was, if this didn't work.

Seem like to Auntee she still just a slave. Just owned by some man. What was all that big Surrender about, all them Blue men on horses, if she still have to be a slave? How do a white man turn blue, anyway? That's one them things she never will know.

Uncle said, "Set down, Mr. Solon, set yourself down, let me see can I find you a clean cup, wrench one out."

Auntee said, "They ain't nothing *but* clean cups in that kitchen, you old white-headed fool. Wrench one out, nothing."

Uncle said, "I'll git it, sho will, you take sugar, Mr. Solon, how do you take your coffee, do you take your coffee sweet?"

Auntee said, "That kitchen is *spotless*."

Solon said, "Well, I couldn't stay."

Auntee poked hurriedly at the fire with an iron poker. Wonder could she ever in this world hit a white man with a poker? Or anybody at all? She set the poker up against the fireplace and pulled up the freshly caned rocker to the hearth.

From the kitchen Uncle said, "Did you say sugar, Mr. Solon?"

Outside, the horn on the El Camino honked.

Solon said, "Let's go, boy."

Uncle said, "Got plenty of sugar."

Solon said, "After we get finished with your boy here, I got some business to take care of with my own family."

Uncle came back into the room with Solon's coffee in a heavy cup.

He said, "*Do?* Well, sah, that's nice, ain't it, nice to hear. You's a family man. I thought you was. Got plans to spend time with your family tonight, is you?"

Solon shifted the two pistols.

He said, "That's right."

Auntee sat in another chair, straight-backed. She folded her hands in her lap.

She said, "Family activities, uh-huh."

Solon said, "They ain't gone be too active, I don't reckon."

She said, "I gots me some cold bread and black strap molasses, if you hongry."

He said, "Go get in the car. We done had enough chit-chat and foot-dragging."

Auntee said, "Oh, Lawd, oh please don't do it."

Uncle said, "Let me give him a whuppin, I'll give him a whuppin he won't forget."

They were down the steps now.

Auntee said, "Oh, Lawd, Mr. Solon, have mercy."

The rain was still falling. Solon opened the car door and the light came on in the ceiling.

Solon said, "This is the one I was telling you about."

Poindexter said, "That's him? That's the one?"

Solon said, "You looking at him."

This time it was a fist.

Poindexter said, "Let's see the picture in your pocket, boy. Let's see that white girl you say is such a good piece of tail."

Solon started up the car and pulled away from Uncle and Auntee's shack.

Poindexter said, "Let's see it. Let's see the picture of the white girl you fucked."

Solon stopped the car on the slick road and left the engine running and switched on the overhead light.

Solon said, "Whoo-ee. They got some good-looking stuff in Chi-car-go, now don't they, Dexter."

Poindexter took the wallet and looked carefully at the photo. He looked at Solon. He said, "Do you know who this is?"

Solon said, "She favors somebody I know, seem like."

Poindexter said, "You goddamn idiot, this is Hedy Lamarr."

Solon took the wallet and looked carefully at the photograph.

Hedy Lamarr. Solon thought he had heard the name.

Poindexter said, "You fucking white-trash fool. You led me to believe that this was a picture of my wife."

Solon said, "Watch who you calling a fool, Dexter."

Poindexter said, "You fucking idiot! That's Hedy Lamarr. Do you even know who Hedy Lamarr is?"

Solon took the German Luger out of his jacket pocket. He held the barrel in Poindexter's face.

He said, "Get out."

Poindexter said, "You deliberately led me to believe that this was a photograph of Sally Anne."

Solon said, "And it wont. It was some other slut instead. Get out, asshole. This is your only invitation."

Poindexter watched his El Camino disappear through the rain. He stood in the drenching rain and wanted to die. He started walking back towards his unhappy home, ten miles through the darkness, across the bridge.

BACK AT the cabin, Auntee picked up the nightshirt Bobo had taken off. She shook the wrinkles out of it and looked at it real hard, critical. There was blood on it, from the first time the pistol butt had cracked down on the boy's head. She folded it and pulled out a basket of dirty clothes and put it on top.

Uncle pulled on his brogans. He said, "I'll walk to the telephone at Sims and Hill, call the High Sheriff."

Auntee said, "Won't do no good."

Uncle said, "I know."

Auntee said, "What's the High Sheriff gone do?"

Uncle said, "I know."

Auntee said, "Get you lynched, is all."

Uncle said, "I know, Auntee."

Auntee said, "Don't go, Uncle. I need you here."

Uncle said, "The world's done changed, Auntee. Ours has. I got to call the High Sheriff, even if it kills me."

Auntee said, "It will. It's near-bout five miles."

Uncle said, "Five miles never kilt nobody."

Auntee said, "Don't go, Uncle."

Uncle said, "Well, I got to."

Auntee said, "You an old man, it's raining so hard."

Uncle said, "I love you, Miss Auntee."

Some time passed. Uncle was gone. Auntee undressed for bed again, put on the cotton-sack nightdress again.

She didn't think she could possibly go to sleep, not until Uncle got back, anyway. But she did, she drifted off.

Then, after a while, she woke up. She thought, "Now what was the name of the horror that I went to sleep upon?"

A long time later, after they had moved away from the Delta and were sleeping in a bed in Chicago, Auntee would say,

"Uncle."

Uncle said, "Whut."

Auntee said, "You know that thing you said?"

Uncle said, "Whut thing?"

Auntee said, "That thing you said about you would be satisfied if somebody would just whup him?"

Uncle said, "Aw, Auntee, don't, now. That was just a way of talking to whitefolks, you know."

Auntee said, "No, I agree. I do. You said the Lawd's truth. Somebody ought to been whupped that child in a inch of his life for pulling this selfish stunt."

Uncle said, "Don't say nothing you gone be sorry about. Let the boy rest."

Auntee said, "I mean it, Uncle. I'm mad at that child. Don't nobody deserve to be murdered, don't even deserve to be whipped for what he done. Whistling at somebody's wife, course not. Plenty men whistle at somebody's wife, don't nothing happen, black or white. But that don't keep me from being mad, don't mean I ain't so mad at him I could about die, I could just about die, what he done, what he done done to all of us."

That would happen a lot later. Now, Auntee was alone in the Delta darkness, with rain on the tin roof.

She slept again, and then, around dawn but not yet light, something outside of her pain woke Auntee up.

It was Uncle's voice—old man voice, low, morning music. Uncle was lying beside her in bed, singing.

She only heard a few lines, before he stopped.

He sang, *I don't want you to cook my bread.*

He sang, *I don't want you to make my bed.*

He sang, *I don't want you cause I'm sad and blue.*

He sang, *I just want to make love to you.*

She said, "I love you, Uncle."

Uncle said, "I love you, Miss Auntee. We done done all that we can do."

7

THE MISSISSIPPI Delta is not always dark with rain. Some autumn mornings, the sun rises over Moon Lake, or Eagle, or Choctaw, or Blue, or Roebuck, all the wide, deep waters of the state, and when it does, its dawn is as rosy with promise and hope as any other.

In autumn, the cornfields have not been plowed under yet, and the old stalks, standing ten feet tall, have turned from green to brown, and in the morning sun they look like solid gold.

Ears of the unharvested crop become full ripe and the husks break open as if a hand, invisible, had shucked them free, and kernels fall loose like coins from a treasure chest, and mourning doves whistle and coo and leave the forest trees and telephone lines and follow the pot of gold at the end of the constant rainbow and become fat on the feast.

And the rice fields, too. What about the rice fields in the beautiful Delta? The mallards approach in their chevron, heads like emerald in the new sun, and the egg-brown dear little hens.

They circle, they drop down, one and then another, they set their wings, which creak and click in the hollow bones against the resisting air, they touch down in the water, they feed, they sleep, they dream.

Begin again, the mallards say, *Begin*, the rice fields whisper, even in drought time from the voices of the pumps, those solitary, electrical songs sucking sweetness from springs and slow streams.

And, in the Delta, in autumn, what do the cottonfields say, when the harvest is done, and the pickers have gone, the mechanical ones, and the human, too? What do the cotton fields say, in the absence of the pilot and his plane, the cropdusters like snake doctors?

What do the cotton fields say when the green leaves are gone, and the square and the blossom and the boll? What do they say, when only the stalks remain, like skinny black girls in ragged dresses of white?

Do they say, *Shouldn't our ancient suffering be more fruitful by now?*

This is what Runt Conroy said to Fortunata on the telephone that night, when the rain was still falling. This is what long memory of the Delta's beauty taught Runt to say to his wife, though the memory was dim and the clouds were still low, and the rain still fell, and Runt still carried an odor of farms and lofts and of the denizens of the earth and air, domestic and wild.

The pay telephone was not in a booth, and it was not

indoors, where a black man might mistake an invitation to make a call on it as an invitation to perform some other, more threatening act of equality; it was stuck on a wall, outside Red's place, not even up under the porch, out in the weather. Runt had a pocketful of quarters. Fortunata was in Kosiesko, he knew where to find her, he didn't ask no questions.

He said, "I miss you. I need you. Come home."

Fortunata was there, he could hear her breathing, but she did not speak.

He said, "I mean, you know that tree, out on the Indian mound, out past Lem Mahoney's place?"

Fortunata said, "Well, yeah—"

He said, "I don't know. Something about that tree, the roots. All those dead Indians and pottery, arrows."

Fortunata revealed no trace of irritation, or even hopelessness, but she did not speak, either.

He said, "I got a bad feeling, honey. I don't know why."

Runt really meant to say that beauty was everything, unless it was only nothing, only the start of the terror that we can probably not bear, or can't imagine bearing, anyway.

Runt said, "It's just so personal, baby. I just never knew how personal the world was, life and all."

Fortunata said, "Cyrus, you're drinking yourself to death. I can't watch it no more."

Cyrus. Nobody had called Runt by his real name in twenty years, thirty maybe. The sound of his own name, like a stranger, like an old book he started reading, once upon a time, and liked it, too, but somehow never got around to finishing.

What was the name of that book? Or maybe it was a poem, something Miss Alberta, his second-grade teacher, read to him one time, long time ago, in another Delta rainstorm, seated with other children on an oiled floor at the schoolhouse, with the steam radiator singing, "Let me call you sweetheart," or some other sentimental tune.

Maybe it was "Hiawatha." *By the shining deep sea waters stood the wigwam of Nacoma, daughter of the moon, Nacoma.*

He said, "That tree is like a habit, you know? The tree on the Indian mound. It's like the rain tonight, it's like the wind. Is it raining in Kosiesko?"

Fortunata said, "I been asleep for hours, Cyrus. I don't know if it's raining or not. What time is it?"

He said, "It's like there's an emptiness inside me."

She said, "Well, I'm not likely to be the one to fill it up. I tried that."

He said, "It's been raining all day and all night. The wind is gnawing at my face."

She said, "Cyrus, you are the only man I ever really loved, but I cain't live with you no more. I'm all give out."

He said, "I don't want to fill up that empty hole no more. I'm through trying."

She said, "Well, you done proved they ain't enough whiskey in the world, or enough Fortunata neither, to fill it up."

He said, "Understand me, baby, listen to me tonight." But he couldn't find the words. He meant to say that he wanted to throw the emptiness inside him out into space. He wanted to say, I want my emptiness outside of me, for once in my life, out in the air we breathe. I want it to fill up the spaces above the cornfields and the rice fields and the cotton fields. I want the mallards to feel it around them when they're flying, I want it to thin out the air they're sailing through, and the doves. I want the engine on the cropduster to stall for a second, my emptiness takes up so much space. He said, "Just come back home. I need you. The kids need you."

She wanted to say, You were always distracted by hope, by romance. She said, "Oh, Cyrus, I don't know, I don't know. I just don't trust you."

He said, "I don't know what I'm going to do, Fortunata. This ain't a plan of action that I'm telling you about, it's a change in the heart, in the soul."

She said, "Well, what then? What am I supposed to think, what am I supposed to do?"

He said, "Ain't our suffering done got old enough? Hadn't it ought to start bearing some decent berries for a durn change?"

WHEN ALICE Conroy was a girl, she didn't believe in magic. She didn't give it a thought. If Alice believed in anything, it was in light and air.

Alice believed in girl-stuff. She liked pink. She liked taffeta and crinoline. She liked petticoats. She told her daddy that "petty," like in "petticoats," meant "little" in the French language. Her daddy said, "Well, parly voo, and pardon yore Franch." Her daddy loved her, but he was hard to get close to.

Alice liked ribbons for her hair. She liked mirrors and brushes and fingernail polish, and even before her mama thought she was old enough for makeup, she bought some makeup anyway, at Woolworth's, and a little glass bottle of Woolworth perfume, too, and her daddy laughed so hard at the way it smelled on her that her mama went on and let her spend her money, which she earned clerking at Mr. Shanker's drug store, on some real, sure enough makeup and a little bottle of real perfume called Evening in Paris. Her daddy said it smelled like an afternoon in Cruger. Her daddy was all time making a joke. She didn't care. She loved her daddy.

Alice had a barrette collection, too. Plastic mostly, but also one made of bone, and one of wood, and another one made out of gen-u-ine mother-of-pearl, which her daddy told her wont nothing but a fancy name for oyster shells. She would just as soon he didn't tell her that.

Also a horse collection, figurines, you know, made out of glass, or plastic, or carved out of wood. When she was a little girl, she would lie in bed at night and dream about having her own pony. She pretended like she woke up one Christmas morning and her daddy had bought her a Pinto pony, sweet-faced, big-eared little tame thing, white with big brown spots, and a leather saddle that creaked.

In the pretend-like daydream she was having, her daddy brought the pony right in the house to surprise her, and was standing in the living room beside the Christmas tree, holding it with a blue bridle when she came in, all sleepy in her nightgown, one Christmas morning, the Christmas-tree lights shining, red and green and white, and an angel up on top of the tree. Well, maybe she did believe in magic, a little bit.

She liked buckle-up shoes, and saddle oxfords, and penny loafers. She liked pink pedal pushers, although she admitted that her daddy was right, they did make her butt look big.

Alice played her share of jacks. She bounced that hard

little red rubber ball. She did her onesies and her twosies, and all the rest. She jumped rope, and double-rope. She knew all the chants. *Ching-chong Chinaman sitting on a fence, trying to make a dollar out of fifteen cents.* She cut out about a million paper dolls, and dressed them up in cut-out clothes, which she was handy at folding back the little white tabs on, so they wrapped all the way around and out of sight, and so the clothes fitted snug and true, even the ones she cut out of the Sears and Roebuck catalog. She made up stories about her dolls, the boys who loved them, the fine cities they visited, or lived in.

Alice loved Little LuLu comic books, especially Little LuLu's private diary, which was always written on the middle two pages of the book.

And there was other stuff she liked that wasn't girl-stuff, not exactly. She loved the light, and the air, of the Mississippi Delta, her home, and the woods, and the fields. Partly she loved them because her daddy loved them, and they were the only things he knew how to share with her without making a joke. Swarms of bees, and honey trees, red clover to the horizon, and white clover, and honeysuckle, and yellow bitterweed, and brindle cows standing chest-deep in black water.

Alice's daddy was not a hunter, and not a farmer, but he took her out in the Delta wilderness to look at the things hunters looked at, and into the fields to look at the things that farmers saw, if hunters and farmers ever really saw the details of their rich lives.

She saw turtles on a log, lazybones, sleeping in the sun, how you gonna git your day's work done; she saw water moccasins on a low branch, all tongue and cotton mouth, wide open with interest in the sound of her voice, as if she were sister to the beauty of slime, and with no evil intent; she saw wild pigs snuffling beneath forest oaks, and their piglets, pink, hairless babydolls, feeding decently, serenely, with delicacy and good manners, on acorns fat with pulp and sweet as apples; she saw deer in the morning, with tails like big white flags and antler racks like rocking chairs for children, and she looked upon their still-warm beds, where spotted fawn had suckled the sleepy doe, and the nervous buck slept with one eye open wide; once she saw a brown bear, old man with a purple tongue, eating dewberries on the edge of the woods, careful to avoid the thorns of the wild and fragrant rose bushes entwined in the same fruit, in the same field.

Maybe this is the reason she fell in love with Dr. Dust, though he was twice her age and as impossible to get close to as her daddy. He looked at things in the same way as her daddy—other things, words mainly, not woods and fields, not bears, but the same, and he showed them to her, those words, poems, as if they were merely wild angels, like the ones she saw feeding quietly at the edge of the woods, in the morning sun, on dewberries, when she was a girl. He made the small world around them extravagant with the praise of words.

The morning she saw the bear, she was with her daddy, of course. She was twelve, maybe thirteen.

She said, "It's like an angel."

They stood a while longer, with the sun rising still, rosy in the east, and they kept on watching from the place by the fence where they had been standing for a long time, by then, there in the darkness, since long before the sun showed itself at all.

In a few moments the bear stopped feeding and stood on all fours for a minute, and then sat back on its big old butt, and scratched behind one ear with its hind foot at a flea, like a big lazy dog.

Her daddy said, "It could kill us with scorn alone."

Alice was thinking these thoughts as she tried to sleep in her bed at Uncle Runt's house. She adjusted her pillow. She gave one real big deep sigh. She lay awake long enough to hear that the rain had let up, maybe even stopped.

She thought about Glenn Gregg in his pitiful home.

She thought of her Uncle Runt. She understood the tragedy of his life.

She thought about Dr. Dust. She imagined that he made vulgar jokes to her in front of his wife.

Her bed was so comfortable, even in the horror of what

she must have sensed, out there in the darkness, on the spillway.

She went back to sleep. There was nothing else she could do, once she understood the futility of magic to change anything of importance in the world.

IN THE summertime, when a nuisance of pecans began to fall off the trees like hail and when pecan sap gummed up windshields and stripped paint from the Chevrolets and Mercuries and DeSotos and Kaisers, and when fig milk poured out of the stems of fallen fruit, Roy Dale was always walking behind the yellow-painted power mower, with a Briggs and Stratton engine that rattle-rattle-rattled through his hands and arms and in his head, and that he bought on time from Mr. Gibson at the Western Auto store.

He leaned into the mower, with his arms and his back and breathed the fragrances of Bermuda and lespedeza and Johnson grass and crab and nut, cutting swaths and then turning and lapping two wheels over the last swath and cutting back down the yard in the opposite direction, of half the yards in Arrow Catcher, Mississippi.

He was dreaming of escape.

To Roy Dale, the lawnmower was freedom from Mississippi. It was dollars—for an illegal quart of beer, sometimes, or a pack of Camels, or an occasional rubber to blow up.

But not just money. Not really money at all, in fact. The yellow-painted Briggs and Stratton lawnmower was a loud-noise silence from which to dream.

Roy Dale suspected that Mississippi was beautiful. He wasn't sure. He didn't have anything to compare it to. He hadn't even ever been out of the Delta.

He had heard about red-clay banks along rivers in the hills, clay as red as blood, somebody told him, colored red with iron in the dirt.

He had heard about deep forests of blue spruce in the hills that, when you walked through them, smelled like sweetened turpentine. Were they really blue?

He had heard about the Gulf Coast, too—white sands, and palm trees, and coconuts, pretty girls in two-piece swimming suits, and green-felt poker tables, and slot machines, and striptease dancers, and comedians right up on a stage telling jokes to you, and wide blue water, stretching out to Ship Island, and Cuba, and Lord knows where-all.

Roy Dale was not good with directions, but he knew north and south and east and west. He had these directions down pat. Behind his lawnmower, with its rattle-rattle-rattle and barrump-barrump-barrump, and with a fragrance of green, fresh-cut grass, and of gasoline and hot motor oil, in his nostrils, Roy Dale would think, All right, west, over there where the sun is going down—that's Texas, that's California.

Cows and gold mines. Cattle drives and stampedes, miners, forty-niners, and my darling Clementine. Coyotes and mesas and motherlodes. He didn't know much, but west was one thing he did know.

These were the things Roy Dale thought about in the summertime, and even in the fall, on Saturdays, when rain wasn't filling up the ditches, and backing up into sewers, and sending big snakes up into the porcelain toilet bowls on the first floors of houses, and making loblollies of every spot of available earth, and even then, sometimes, he thought about these things, like today, this late night, in his room alone in bed, fingering the fletching of an arrow from the quiver the coach let him bring home before practice on Monday morning.

8

SOLON WAS leaning down over the steering wheel, trying to see where he was going in all this rain. He was sitting up on the front edge of his seat like a child, trying to keep the El Camino from slipping off in a ditch. The headlights were poking out through the rain, the rain was drumming on the roof and in the truck bed.

Solon said, "Once we get up to the gravel, we'll be able to make a little better time, visibility won't be so bad."

They drove on a while longer, in silence.

Solon said, "I ain't never driving down this slick durn road again."

Then Solon said, "Here we go! Here's the gravel! All right! Man! I thought we's lost there for a minute."

He pulled the truck up onto the gravel and turned left, headed out into Runnymede.

He said, "Well, shoot! That's a relief. Shit far."

Solon could lean back into the backrest a little, now that they had made the high road. He could see better, relax a little. The windshield wipers were going zoop zoop zoop.

Solon said, "I'd done got myself a little tense there for a minute."

Solon was able to get up a little speed now, on the better

road. The sound of the wet gravel beneath the tires was like
bacon sizzling in a frying pan.

On the better road, Solon didn't mind taking his hand
off the wheel for a couple of seconds. He reached into his
back pocket and took out a crumpled white handkerchief
and handed it over.

He said, "It ain't too durn clean."

Solon got to the spillway and stopped. The lights shone
across the water, which was high now, on account of the
rain. Lake water had covered the road, which was also the
high water dam, and was spilling over it into the gum
swamp in a long white line of frothy water.

Solon said, "I wonder can I drive across this durn thing."

They sat in the truck, with the motor running. The water
poured over the spillway like music. The headlights were
like long yellow planks in the darkness, stretched across the
spillway to the other side.

Solon said, "I heard this is a good place to fish, the
spillway."

Solon waved off the bloody handkerchief.

He said, "Just keep it."

They drove on for a while, across Runnymede.

He said, "You ever go fishing?"

Solon imagined fish beneath the dam, silent and silver in
the dark.

He took a breath and let it out. He said, "I'm always

thinking I'm going to go fishing sometime myself, and then I don't."

He said, "I seen all them fishing poles back at the house. Uncle, he got plenty of fishing poles, don't he? What's Uncle do, cut him some cane poles out in the brake, dry them out in the rafters?"

Dark night, and the rain kept on drumming on the roof of the El Camino, but Solon thought it wont such a bad night for a drive, for sitting out in a car with a boy and listening to the falling water on the tin roof.

He said, "What do you reckon your Uncle would charge me for a good fishing pole? You and me, maybe we'll get together, go fishing some time, what'da you think? Wet us a couple of hooks, you know."

Solon reached in his pocket and took out the thousand dollars, the big fat roll of new bills.

He said, "Reckon that ought to be enough for two fishing poles?" He held it out for inspection.

He laughed a quiet laugh.

He said, "This ought to buy us a couple of pretty good poles, oughtn't it? First-rate fishing poles. Throw in a Prince Albert can full of nightcrawlers to boot, don't you reckon?"

Solon rolled down his window and sat for a couple of minutes holding the money. Then he flung the roll of bills out into the wind and rain and rolled the window back up again.

The bills went every which-away at first, and then the rain sogged them down, out on the road and in the ditch and some of them blew into the spillway and over the dam, and out into the water of the lake.

He had a second thought, then, so he rolled his window back down, and took the .25 caliber pistol from out the front of his pants and slung it out the window, too, backhand, out in the rain. No telling where it landed, somewhere off the road, someplace, or in the ditch, or out in the field.

The water was pouring over the dam, making its musical sound, different from the rain on the roof, though that sound was like music, too.

Solon said, "Do you reckon I could drive across the top of this thing?"

He rolled his window back up again.

Solon said, "Trouble is, that spillway current is so durn strong, it's liable to push this little truck right off in Roebuck Lake."

They sat for a while longer without talking.

He said, "You know what I ought to of did, don't you? I ought to of insisted that he find that slut wife of his and give me the Cadillac, instead of this candyass contraption.

This durn El Camino ain't all it's cracked up to be, once the novelty's done wore off. That's my own personal opinion."

A long time passed, then. Solon looked at the dashboard lights. They were green and comfortable-looking, they made Solon consider that his life was in good order. Good oil pressure. Radiator, not a bit of overheating. Fuel— well. The fuel was a little low, not bad, though. Solon hadn't thought to check his gas gauge, back at Sims and Hill. He could have told Hydro, "Fill 'er up," if he'd of thought about it. Look like now he was running a little low, nothing to worry about.

He said, "You know another thing I never did that I always wanted to? Before I die, I wish I could dig me up some fresh peanuts out the ground and soak them in brine, real salty, you know, boil them good, and then roast them somehow, like on that iron stove in your Auntee's kitchen. I don't know why digging up my own fresh peanuts always appealed to me. It's just one of them durn things."

The music of the spillway water in the swamp sounded like soft, faraway plucking on the strings of the guitars of the blues singers on Red's front porch.

Solon said, "I'm pretty much committed to crossing this durn thing. I ought to just go on and do it. I don't know what I'm waiting on."

He laughed again, his soft laugh.

He kept looking out into the darkness, along the plane

made by the headlights, across the spillway, towards a barn that was still too far away to see.

Solon said, "See, I always kind of thought I would take my boy fishing, someday, the one what got burnt up. Two cane poles with bream hooks, cat-gut line, and red-and-white plastic bobbers, little piece of lead shot. Maybe dig some worms, trap some roaches, seine some minnows."

The cypress swamp that the water flowed into was black, black, and the gum trees were full of sleeping swamp birds, blue herons, and long-legged cranes and turkey vultures and snowy egrets and kingfishers.

He said, "Down in New Orleans, guess what I did. You won't never guess it in a million years. I'll tell you. I slept in a bed same day a man died in it, didn't even change the sheets."

Then, what the hail?

At first Solon didn't quite know what happened.

Rain was blowing into the El Camino.

Where'd all that durn wind and rain come from? That was the first thought that come into his head. He checked his window, see had he rolled it up real good.

Then he said, "Oh."

He said, "Oh, I see. Bobo has done struck out on his own."

He thought, Well, I swanee. Ain't that the limit? We's just sitting here having us a friendly conversation, and first thing I find out, straight out of the clear blue, that boy ain't even been listening. I knowed he was awful quiet, I ought to been done remarked on the rudeness of him letting me do all the talking, and goddurn it all if I ain't feeling the least bit foolish right about now, finding out he wont even-down listening. And you know what else?—that door opened just easy as pie, didn't it? I didn't even hear it click. Wont one bit of trouble getting out that door, was it? Well, it's a new car, it's to be expected. Ole Dexter his ownself could have jumped out that door any time he wanted to, if he'd of just thunk of it.

In a way it was like going to sleep for Solon, when he caught on that Bobo had made his move, left the car. It was like finally dropping off to sleep, when you're just so durn tired you just bout to die. What a relief. That's what Solon was thinking. It's over. Thank-you-jesus. It's all over.

Solon wondered about Bobo, out there in the rain, in that gravel. Sharp rocks he's running on, just got to be. He hoped it was easier on his feet than it looked like, sho did. He spected that road gravel had clay in it, he spected Bobo had done sunk up over his shoes in red clay. First step, one shoe sucked off, next step, other shoe. That's what Solon was thinking. Cain't be no fun, dying without your shoes on, rocks on your heels, mud like quicksand, rainwater standing up on that bloody little meat-raw nappy head of his like pearls, like a crown of jewels. Got to be uncomfortable, sho does, even for a nigger.

And you want to know something else Solon was about to mention to that boy before he showed this unexpected rude streak? He was about to say to him that, in a way, he wont sure quite how, Bobo reminded Solon a little bit of Jesus. Well, it was a compliment, if you looked at it in the right way.

It wont Jesus, exactly, that Bobo put him in mind of. It was one of them little plaster of Paris Jesuses, like you see sometimes riding up on the dashboard of a car. Now why do you reckon Bobo's gone remind Solon of a plastic Jesus, colored child like he was and Jesus white as the day is long? Solon didn't claim to have no analytical mind, he just meant to pay the boy a compliment, if he wanted to take it that way.

Seem like there was a song about plastic Jesus, wont they? Solon looked around in his head for the tune. He sang, *I don't care if it rains or freezes*. He couldn't remember the rest. Something about a plastic Jesus, though.

Well, sure, that was it. Bobo the Plastic Jesus, sho nuff. Solon wondered had anybody else ever noticed the resemblance.

So Solon sho did hate for Bobo to be out there behind the truck, scared half out of his wits and cutting his feet on sharp gravel, just because he was taking him out to kill him. It was a shame, a crime and a shame.

And dark out there, too, don't you spect? Pore thang, blind in that Delta darkness, don't you just know he is, cain't see a blessed thing, don't know where he's running to. Breathing like a bellows, like somebody tearing up clean rags in his chest.

That's what Solon thought, was thinking. Got to be awful for the boy, ready to breathe his last breath like he was, sho does, jess awful.

When's he gone realize it's over, Solon was thinking. When he gets around back to the tailgate? When he's laying out in a ditch, or a field, or up inside a hollowed-out gum stump, waiting for me to come find him? When he realizes they ain't no protection against this big pistol, down under the car seat, that well's to been born in this hand of mine?

Okay, so when the first bullet hit Solon in the face, it took him a minute to figure out just what the hail had done happened. Well, it was so durn fast, see, that was the thing. First he just sat there musing, like he was, and friendly thoughts, too, sho was, he liked the boy, now that he'd done spent some time talking with him, getting to know him.

When the bullet split his jaw open and knocked out some teeth and cut off the end of his tongue, he wondered if he didn't look to Bobo a little bit silly, maybe a little self-satisfied, thinking he was so well in control of the situation. He wondered if he didn't look to Bobo like he was saying, "Huh? What? Who done shot me in the face?" It was embarrassing, Solon didn't have no trouble admitting that much. It took him a minute or two to collect his wits, on account of being so durn surprised.

What Solon reckoned was, the boy must of found that durn pistol that Solon throwed out the car window, Bobo must of, that's what Solon finally started to figure out. Bobo must of had his sights on that pistol all the time, seen it glinting some place out there in the black darkness, in the weeds, Lord knows how, not even a nickel-plated pistol, and no moon at all, but he must of done that, somehow another, seen it out there in the weeds, or the ditch, and me sitting up here in this sissified car talking about fishing poles and boiled peanuts, and well don't I feel like a solid gold fool. I must be blushing, bound to be.

Up under the front seat, that's where the heavy pistol was laying, the German Luger. Solon had tucked it there when he got back in the truck at Uncle and Auntee's house. He reached down and touched it with his hand.

The second shot flashed out, back behind him, just over Solon's left shoulder, and this one hit him in the neck. He slumped down in the seat.

The third shot hit the door of the truck, and missed Solon altogether.

The next shot was worse, didn't even hit the truck, that boy's losing his touch.

Then the next one hit him high on the left side, and Solon thought, "Well, now I know what it sounds like when a rib breaks. It sounds like a banjo string, real bad out of tune." This was the shot that turned him right over on the seat, flop.

Shock, it's not such a bad thing, really, shock ain't, medical terminology, you know, what you all-time hear about somebody going into when they get hurt real bad. It's an overused term, akshully, shock is. Somebody's all-time declaring, "I like to done went into shock!" Shock's not no mystery, though. It's about like most any other illness you might be unlucky enough to get. It ain't so bad. You don't feel nothing at all, once the shock gets going real good. The blood pressure, it goes way down, all of a sudden. Body temperature, the same. Breathing gets real slow, heartbeat, slow as molasses, liver function, kidney function, not much, I'm telling you. It's a way of protecting you from pain, you ought to be grateful for shock, don't be complaining to me about it, shock is your friend.

The problem with shock, though, see, is you can die of it, shock gets serious, after a while.

Solon, though, he didn't go into shock. Some do, some don't. Unpredictable, see, shock is. Solon always knowed there was some good reason for having that lightweight little peashooter pistol of his. You can get shot a half-dozen times with that durn little popgun and you still won't go into shock.

Different story, now, with a heavy pistol, big caliber handgun like a Luger, sho now. You get shot one or two times with that sapsucker, you gone go into shock whether you want to or not.

Solon didn't look too durn good, with his teeth and tongue missing, the way they suddenly was, he wasn't denying that—but he didn't go into shock.

In fact, he got off a few shots his ownself, right before he passed out, in the direction of the flame that shot out of the little gun barrel, out there in the dark swamp, in the weeds with the rain still falling in sheets.

Long time after this night was over and done with, Bobo's mama, up in Chicago, out by the viaduct where the Blood Rangers wore berets and wrote their names in spraypaint on the viaduct, she wondered who Bobo was thinking about that night, those couple of minutes there in the swamp-grass, with bullets flying in all directions.

She wondered was he thinking about her, his mama, who raised him up and loved him and wiped his rear end and gave him some titty when he was a hongry baby, and fed him some Gerber's cereal and beets, and took him to the doctor when he was sick, and when he needed his booster shots, and looked all over Chicago for some little books to read to him that had pictures of colored children in them, and went over his spelling words with him before the test, and taught him how to hold his fork and his knife, and cried when some sassy little bitch wearing a skirt with pink bows all the way around the hem wouldn't dance with him at the Valentine's party in the school cafeteria because he talked with a teeny-tiny little lisp.

Probably not, boy-child like Bobo, spote like he was, his daddy dead and gone. Bobo's mama reckoned her boy probably wasn't thinking about her a-tall, even though she was the one who would live a long time after this and would say words with meanings that her friends didn't have no way of knowing what they meant to her, like, "Be sure to put the milk back in the refrigerator so it don't spoil," or "Somebody take that bone away from the dog."

Bobo's mama thought Bobo was probably thinking about his daddy, who he never knew. Whose big gold ring he was wearing on his finger, that dark night among the gum stumps, in the rain, when the first bullet knocked out his eye and the second one dislocated his shoulder.

9

FROM THE eye that Solon's bullet had knocked from its socket and that hung now upon the child's moon-dark cheek in the insistent rain, the dead boy saw the world as if his seeing were accompanied by an eternal music, as living boys, still sleeping, unaware, in their safe beds, might hear singing from unexpected throats one morning when they wake up, the wind in a willow shade, bream bedding in the shallows of a lake, a cottonmouth hissing on a limb, the hymning of beehives, of a bird's nest, the bray of the iceman's mule, the cry of herons or mermaids in the swamp, and rain across wide water. In this music the demon eye saw what Bobo could not see in life, transformations, angels and devils, worlds invisible to him before death.

He saw Solon wake up in the front seat of the truck spitting blood. He saw him struggle to sit up, to get his bearings, clear his head. He saw him leave the truck, limping in the rain with the heavy pistol in his hand, a bullet in his left arm, teeth missing. Bobo watched him check the body in the grass, Bobo's own dead body, the body seeing its own murderer from a demon and immortal eye.

He saw him turn away, enter the truck, drive away again, careless across the spillway waters, which foamed up white against the wheels of the little truck, and the running board and the door with one bullet hole in the glass and two more in the metal, those heavy, tuneful, humorous waters that tugged at the little truck and tried to tip it into the stream and did not succeed, though for fractions of a second the truck rose up from the dam on dark liquidity and was supported only by swamp, the second time today Solon had walked on water.

Through the demon eye he saw Solon, tense behind the steering wheel, holding the truck on its true course until he reached the safety of the other side, rain still falling like pennies from heaven, dirty copper, the headlights, demon eyes themselves, laying beams like gangplanks on a pirate ship.

He saw Solon, a few miles further down the road, switch off the lights and ease the little truck into a farmyard, across a cattle-gap and through a fence, taking a chance on getting stuck in the mud out by the barn. Solon was stealing a weight, a gin fan, and a length of barbed wire to tie the fan to Bobo's neck, to sink the body in the stream.

Oh, there was music in the swamp, the irrigation pumps in the rice paddies, the long whine and complaint, the wheezy, breathy asthma of the compress, the suck and bump and clatter like great lungs as the air was squashed out and the cotton was wrapped in burlap and bound

with steel bands into six-hundred-pound bales, the bark-
ing of a collie-rat, a swamp-elf singing in a cabbage
patch, an old man clogging on a bridge, geese arriving
from Canada, a parrot ringing like a cash register, mos-
quitoes like violins, the wump-wump-wump-wump-wump
of cropdusters, mourning doves in the walnut trees.

Solon let down the tailgate of the El Camino. He knew
just where to find the gin fan, back in the tool area of the
barn. It was a big, greasy, rusted fan, out of the Quito gin.
It was going to be heavy, a hundred pounds or more, he
was glad he had the El Camino. He'd hate to have to put
that big motherfucker in the trunk of Poindexter's Cadillac, especially with a bullet in one arm and a serious dental
problem. If he was in the Cadillac, he'd just have to call the
whole thing off.

Solon had seen the fan when he was stealing refund gas
from the farmer's tank a year or more ago. If he had had
good sense he would have waited to kill Bobo until after
they had this fan in the truck. Bobo could have done the
heavy lifting, big boy like he was. Or they could have
picked it up together, anyhow. It wont logical for a man
Solon's age to be lifting a hundred pounds of steel when
there was a strapping young man like Bobo nearby.

Bobo, dead, back at the spillway in the rain, where he
waited for Solon, could see all this through the demon eye

upon his cheek, without fear or anger, or even a sense of injustice, but only with an appreciation of the dark and magical and evil world in which he had been killed.

The gin fan was both the weight to hide Bobo's body and an object of Bobo's love. In death, his hands reached across the Delta flatscape and touched the fan, where Solon struggled in the rain. Across the distance, Bobo helped buoy it and ease its weight as Solon lifted it into the bed of the pickup.

In death, Bobo saw the gin where the fan had come from, in the little community of Quito, where it had sucked raw cotton, Egyptian or Sea Island fibers, from the trailers and into the dryers, or maybe where it blew seeds off the comb, or de-seeded lint into the wagons headed towards the compress, to be crushed into bales. Quito was a community of mystics, a thousand green snakes on a hoodoo woman's table, Great Danes with blank eyes, walking through walls.

He saw all this, and chocolate milk and cinnamon toast and cold sweet potatoes on Auntee's sideboard, and tupelo gums and cypress and chinaberry and weeping willow and mimosa and a beautiful creature of some kind, a mermaid, maybe, as she rose up from the water, her breasts bare, and combing her long hair with a comb the color of bone, and holding in the other hand a mirror as dark and fathomless as the mirror-surface of Roebuck Lake, and Bobo knew that this mermaid was himself.

Solon was already running a fever by the time he got back to Bobo. Or he seemed to be, his hands were so warm on the child's dead-cold ankles, which he grabbed to pull Bobo out of the field where he died and to the El Camino on the road. Bobo's body slid along, over the saw grass, through the Johnson grass, his head bump-bumping against irregular places in the earth. Bobo lay in the gravel at the rear end of the truck, free of pain and fear.

Solon was clumsy getting the body into the bed of the truck, up beside the gin fan. He heaved and strained. He dropped the body several times. He was making a lot of noise. He said, "Goddamn." He changed positions. The arm with the bullet in it was almost useless to him. Finally he lifted Bobo up by the waist and flung the top half of his body over the tail of the truck. It stayed put. Solon was breathing very hard. The rain was pouring down on his head.

When he had rested for a few minutes, he lifted Bobo's feet from where they hung down out of the truck's bed, and swung them around to the side and up into the truck, blam. The body was in, now, a little precariously perched, but in the bed. So that was good.

Solon slammed shut the tailgate and hooked it, so Bobo wouldn't spill out when he moved the truck. This job was worth a lot more than a thousand dollars, even if he hadn't thrown the money away. Solon had forgotten all about his big plans to end his family's misery, he was too durn tired and wounded to think about anything, much.

He picked up the length of barbed wire that he had stolen from the barn when he took the fan. Bobo watched Solon pull one end of the wire between parts of the fan and then twist and twist the wire until that end was secure. By now Solon's hands were bleeding. Solon hated Bobo. He might have been unclear on this point before, but now he was not. He knew that Bobo's eye was looking at him. He said, "Whut yew lookin at?" Bobo said nothing in return, of course. Then Solon did the same thing with the remaining end of the wire that he had done with the first, but this end he wrapped around Bobo's neck. He twisted and twisted until it was secure. The barbs dug into Bobo's dead flesh and Adam's apple.

For the third time that night, Solon pulled the El Camino onto the spillway, its swift waters beneath the wheels. Bobo's body jolted in the back. It felt the truck lift up from the dam and then settle back down and ease outwards towards the middle of the spillway, white water surging around it.

The demon eye, hanging from its socket down Bobo's cheek, saw a young schoolteacher. She was walking home from school, her heart filled with sadness. In this woman's heart Bobo saw the pain of hopeless love, he saw Solon's child disfigured in his bed, he saw the Spanish moss in the trees outside a Mexican mansion. He saw Alice Conroy see his own dead body in a raindrop. He saw a crystal ball, lost in the depths of Swami Don's Elegant Junk, light up with blue light and an image of things to come. He saw a mojo waving good-bye, one tiny black finger at a time, *good-bye, dear Bobo, we'll never forget you, you'll live forever in our hearts.*

And then he was in the water. First the fan, splash, rolling, rolling, rolling with the strong current along the swamp floor, and then himself, pulled behind, twisting and twisting on his barbed-wire tether, in the swift spillway waters of Roebuck Lake. Solon had somehow gathered the strength to throw him in.

Sliding past him, beneath the black water, he saw an ancient tangle of briers and cypress knees and gum stumps. He saw a billion strings of vegetation and tiny root systems. He saw fish—bright bluegills and silvery crappie, long-snouted gar, and lead-bellied cat with ropy whiskers. He saw turtles and mussels and the earth of plantations sifted there from other states, another age, through a million ditches and on the feet of turkey vultures and blue herons and kingfishers. He saw schools of minnows and a trace of slave death from a century before. He saw baptizings and drownings. He saw the transparent wings of snake doctors, he saw lost fish stringers and submerged logs, a submerged boat, and the ghosts of lovers.

After a long time, the big fan stopped rolling. It came

to a halt, far out in the lake in deep water, and Bobo's body floated decently alongside it, attached by the neck by a length of barbed wire.

Already two weeks had passed. Already the rain, that had so recently insisted it would never stop, was finished, forgotten. The sun shone. Children had attended school for ten days. Already blues singers avoided Red's big front porch. Already Bobo's mother's heart was broken with fear. Already his uncle and auntee's lives were changed forever. Bobo's flesh grew soft in the running water. It lost its rich color. Turtles and fish nibbled at rags of meat. Already the barbed wire tether had slipped and lengthened, and Bobo's feet stuck up out of the water, above the surface of the lake.

Already it was the morning that his body would be found, Sunday in September. Because he was magic now, Bobo saw the two white boys who would find him.

First he saw Sweet Austin, in a johnboat, running trot-lines. Freckle-faced, skinny little white boy. He saw Sweet scull the boat with a Feather paddle. He felt the good sun on Sweet's shoulders. He saw him ease the boat along the trotline, lifting first one hook and then the next, eyeing the hooks critically, replacing the bait if it had been eaten away, as his own flesh had been eaten and changed. He watched Sweet Austin find the body.

Bobo even saw Sugar Mecklin, the housepainter's boy,

in his home, as he slept this bright morning in the dreamy belief that today would turn out to be a special day, unlike any other in his life.

Bobo entered Sugar's dream. In it Sugar stood at the end of a short pier, and Bobo became a mermaid, a bare-breasted creature combing her hair with a comb the color of bone. The white boy woke up, he leaped from his bed and dressed hurriedly and ran down to the real-life pier on the lake bank and stood and scanned the waters with this innocent hope in his heart.

Bobo called out from his death to Sugar, *I am the mermaid that you will love.*

Bobo saw Sweet Austin arrive, the other white boy, who had already spotted Bobo's own decayed feet sticking up from the water.

He saw Sweet come up behind Sugar on the pier. He saw them speak, frightened children.

Sweet said, "Hey, Sugar Mecklin."

Sugar said, "Hey, Sweet Austin."

Sweet Austin said, "I've got to show you something. Something bad."

From his rotted throat Bobo sang along with a choir on the far side of the lake. It was a baptizing. The choir had a friend in Jesus. God's grace was amazing, they said, and sweet. There was a church in the wildwood, they said.

There'll be no sadness, the choir promised, *no trouble, no trouble I see*. Bobo's voice was as sweet as the voice of an angel, which is what a mermaid is, in water not air.

His song—it must have been the magical music of his voice—drew the two white boys together down the lake bank for a few yards to Sweet's boat, which was pulled up into the weeds in a clear spot between the cypress knees.

Sweet Austin stuck the paddle into the gummy leaf-moldy bottom of the lake and used it like a raft pole to shove the boat away from the bank, and Bobo's song, like a magic carpet, eased them away from the shore and out into the deeper water.

The white boys spotted the bare feet and legs sticking up out of the water, where Bobo was snagged in the brush.

Beneath the water, far into his death, Bobo sang, *I am the mermaid, I am the lake angel, I am the darkness you have been looking for all your sad lives*.

Bobo knew that these two boys heard his song and believed it was only the voice of the spillway, its rushing water over concrete and cypress. White cranes stood in small gossipy groups along the shallow water. Turkey vultures sailed like hopeful prayers above them in the wide blue sky and then settled into the empty branches of white-trunked, leafless trees.

Deep in the water fish swam everywhere, invisible to all but Bobo, bream and perch and bass, silver and gold and

blue, all their familiar coloration and feathery gills and lidless eyes, deep comfort to the murdered child who was now
their friend and their food.

It would be a while before this body was properly identified. At first, somebody said it was probably a certain old
colored man who had been missing for a day or two, and
after another day the old man turned up at his son's house
in Moorehead.

In death, Bobo was patient. He had no care for quick
identification. Soon enough, they would see the weight,
they would see the wire, the bullet holes, the magic eye.

From his death Bobo loved the two boys in the boat
above him. Most of all he loved Sweet Austin, who found
him. Bobo saw Sweet's mama working late behind the bar
at the American Legion Hut tonight. She turned on the
switch that caused the Miller High Life sign to revolve.
She borrowed herself a little handful of nickels from the
cash drawer and dropped them, one-two-three, in the one-
armed bandit next to the piano, and every time it come up
lemons, and she said, "Shoot." She reached into the cooler
for long-necked beers in dark bottles, maybe Pabst Blue
Ribbon, or Falstaff, or Jax, or even Pearl, and cracked them
open with a church key, and brushed ice shavings off one
of them for herself, and said to Al the boogie-woogie piano
player, "You buying, ain't you, amigo?"

Bobo knew Sweet's mama would not come home on this

night when Sweet needed her most, not until after the white boy was already deep in his horrible sleep. Bobo knew that she would finally come in, though, and although she was drunk she would manage to turn the key in the front door lock for safety and put the key up on the mantlepiece and sniff around the space heater for gas, to see was it leaking again. She would stagger a little in the hallway, and then prop herself up against the wall and take off her shoes. She would go into the room where her son slept on a steel bunk bed and wake up Sweet Austin and tell him, "I'm home, sweetning, I ain't drunk, ain't even smoked no cigarettes," and then she would crawl in right alongside Sweet Austin on the steel bunk and wake up with some kind of taste in her mouth like she been chewing tin foil out of a gum wrapper, and sore teeth, and no energy to apologize to her boy or anybody else, for all her regret.

Bobo sang, *Don't look, don't look at me, preserve your innocence another moment longer*.

Sweet Austin dragged the paddle in a sculling motion and turned the boat in the direction of a camp-landing a little farther on. He dipped the paddle deep into Roebuck and caused the boat beneath them to move steadily across the lake. Bobo watched them pull away.

He could have watched them dock at the fish camp, he could have seen Mr. Raney look for his glasses to make the call to the High Sheriff. He could have watched Hydro,

Mr. Raney's son, lick peach filling off the palms of his hands
and say, "It's probably the nigger Mr. Solon and Mr. Dexter
done kilt." He could have watched Big Boy Chisholm drive
both boys away from the fish camp and stop the patrol car
out by the iron fence in front of Sugar's house and say, "I'm
sorry y'all boys had to bear witness to that floater, I truly
am sorry."

There was much that Bobo still could have seen through
the magical eye, but now Bobo had stopped seeing. This
part was finished. Now Bobo was dead and gone.

And so this was the day two white boys found a tattered
corpse in the spillway waters of Roebuck Lake in Arrow
Catcher, Mississippi.

10

THE BOW that Roy Dale Conroy had fallen in love with was a six-foot, double-laminated, recurved number, forty-pound test, from the high school's athletic locker. Coach Wily Heard let him bring it home at night and on week-ends.

The bow wasn't new, it had some cracks in the fiberglass, but it was fine, and the bow string was brand new, right out of the package, bright as a dollar.

Coach Heard was a one-legged man, lost one leg in Korea, shrapnel, and had a fiberglass replacement job that he wore on his stump to teach Civics.

In addition to that, he owned an old-fashioned peg leg, tapered to the bottom, with a rubber-tipped flange on the end. He wore the peg to arrow-catching practice, it was a little more comfortable, gave him a sense of stability on the grass, he told people.

Coach Heard kept a half-pint nipper of Old Grand-Dad in his pocket at all times, even up at the schoolhouse. He didn't care much about Civics. He filled up most of his class time talking about Korea. Coach Heard drank whis-key with Roy Dale's daddy down at Red's Goodlookin Bar and Gro. sometimes.

Roy Dale dearly and truly loved this bow and arrow, he'd been sleeping with it for two weeks. Coach Heard had taught him how to string it the right way.

Out on the practice field the first day, Coach Heard said, "Forty-pound test might be a little stout for you at first, but you'll grow into it, and it's all I got to offer right now."

Roy Dale said, "I like it."

Roy Dale watched Coach Heard set the peg-leg flange firmly in the earth. He watched Coach Heard bend the bow evenly between his good foot and the inside of his knee and then slip the loop of the bowstring into the nock, the notch at the end of the bow.

Coach Heard said, "Can you do that?"

Roy Dale said, "I own no."

Coach Heard said, "Well, let's see."

He instructed Roy Dale in the beauty and danger of arrows, tip, shaft, and fletching, and the signal feather, its distinctive color, which always pointed outward from the bow, and how to nock the arrow, to fit it on the string, and how to lay the shaft upon the bow.

He showed him how to raise the bow while drawing the string, how to sight down the arrow, how to estimate and allow for distance and drop and wind, how to breathe, how to have all the work of pulling done before his right hand held and then released beside his right ear.

He called Roy Dale an archer, and when he did, a great

wealth of good feeling burst out of Roy Dale's eyes as tears. Coach Heard pretended not to notice the tears, and then he took Roy Dale back to his office and showed him, in a glass bowl on his desk, a swamp plant called *Sagittara latifolia*, with arrowhead-shaped leaves and white flowers.

Coach Heard held Roy Dale stiffly around the shoulder for a few seconds, propped a little to the left, as he normally did, to take some weight off his stump, which was often tender, though he didn't complain.

Coach Heard said, "I read this book one time about archery and Zen, you ever hear about it? You ever heard of Zen? I got it around the house somewhere, if I can find it, maybe I'll bring in, let you borrow it for a while, take a look-see. You'd have to return it, though, don't lose it or spill nothing on it, okay?"

So Roy Dale had been sleeping with the bow and the cracked-leather quiver of arrows for two weeks.

Each night in his room he strung and unstrung and re-strung the bow. Not for practice—he had done it perfectly the first time, it was a natural movement of his hand and foot and knee—but only to feel the powerful core of it, the grave potentialities of its heart, the unsung and waiting angel-music of its string.

The arrows, there were eight of them, he laid out on his bed like pick-up sticks. He stirred them upon the wool blanket with his hand, to hear the soft percussion of the wood.

He arranged them in a line, all the tips pointing in the same direction. He picked each arrow up, held it, ran his hand along the shaft, its whole length, ran his thumb upon the coarse plastic of each feather of the fletching, gripped the arrow tight in the middle of the shaft, held it high above his head like a prize.

He bought neat's foot oil at Mr. Shanker's Drug Store, a small glass vial for a quarter, and with his bare hand he rubbed the oil into the worn-out leather of the quiver, and softened it some, and made it dark, dark. He breathed the fragrant oil into his nostrils like a memory, or desire, he exhaled it like a prayer, he rubbed the oil from his hands onto his face, and into his hair.

Seven of the arrows were competition models, called "blunts," especially designed for amateur catchers, with hard-rubber tips for safety. These Roy Dale shot in the direction of one of his partners, another kid who had made the team, an arrow catcher, usually Sugar Mecklin or Sweet Austin, whose job was to pluck the flash of thickened atmosphere from its element before it struck.

It was dangerous. Arrow catchers required a gift, a certain temperament, more than the archer, really, though the archer was important, too. It was a team effort, Coach

Heard insisted, a sloppy archer could injure even the most skilled catcher.

Nobody ever got killed trying to catch a blunt, but concussions, a broken rib, these were possible. A law was pending before the Mississippi legislature to require protective devices for the eyes.

The other arrow, the eighth, was in the quiver by mistake. It was an old thing, with a slight warp in the shaft, left over from the olden days, before the war, when Arrow Catcher High still had a conventional archery program, with bullseye targets set up on hay bales. The eighth arrow had a steel tip—not a hunting blade, a "razor," they were called, only a sharp point, but dangerous nevertheless.

This arrow, at night, sometimes, Roy Dale fitted into the nock and drew back on the string and, despite the warp in the shaft that must have made it wobble in its flight, drove it straight into the wall of his room, smack, deep in the wood.

Sometimes it was the Sheriff of Nottingham, his bedroom wall, and Roy Dale imagined himself wearing a green suit and a feathered cap and having a friend named Little John and looking like Errol Flynn, with good teeth.

And other times it was General Custer, and Roy Dale imagined a loincloth and paint and a spotted horse. He imagined wide deserts and cactus plants.

And sometimes it was something else, nothing that Roy

Dale recognized, no person, and no thing, and even the arrow was not an arrow, but only something from inside himself, some abstraction requiring sudden and violent expulsion, expression, before it killed him, a representation of landscapes of the broken heart, hopeless dreams, a vastness of sorrow that outside of himself might be seen as beautiful and strange, but that inside of him was only poison and filth.

He laid the unstrung bow and the quiver of arrows, blunts and the tipped arrow together, lengthwise in his bed at night, his narrow cot, beneath the coarse blanket, and slept there with them in the comfort of shared dreams.

Roy Dale imagined, sometimes, in these quiet, hopeful hours, that one day he might lie like this, in intimate communion, with a wife, a partner of the heart.

On this particular morning, a school day, Roy Dale noticed that something was wrong with Runt, his daddy. Runt had visited Red's Goodlookin Bar and Gro. already, and Roy Dale could smell alcohol on his breath, but he was not drunk, nowhere close. So that was not the problem.

Roy Dale said, "Hey, Runt."

Runt was sitting at the kitchen table, with his head down on his arms, on the oilcloth. He looked up.

He said, "Hey. I called myself letting you sleep in."

Roy Dale said, "I been up for a while. Coach Heard don't let you practice if you miss school."

Runt said, "Hey, Roy Dale?"

Roy Dale said, "Uh-huh."

Runt said, "How much trouble would it be for you to call me something else besides Runt?"

Roy Dale said, "Well—"

Runt said, "I was just wondering if, you know, you reckon you mought start calling me by some other name than Runt. I done got tired of being called Runt."

Roy Dale said, "You're tired of being called Runt?"

Runt said, "Well, yeah." He said, "Your mama's coming home from Kosiesko tomorrow."

Roy Dale said, "Uh-huh. Well—"

Runt said, "She can spell you and Alice with the young'uns, anyways."

Roy Dale said, "Uh-huh."

Runt said, "They already gone, the chillen. Alice got everybody off to school early this morning."

Roy Dale said, "Well—"

Runt said, "Anyways, give some thought to what I told you, you know, that name business, see can you come up with anything, something else besides Runt."

Roy Dale said, "Uh-huh, okay, yeah."

Runt said, "My real name is, you know, Cyrus."

Roy Dale said, "Cyrus, uh-huh."

Runt said, "You knew that."

Roy Dale said, "Uh-huh, yeah, I think I knew that."

Runt said, "I'd appreciate it, sho would."

Roy Dale said, "Okay."

Runt said, "Mama's gone start calling me Cyrus."

Roy Dale said, "Uh-huh."

Runt said, "It's kind of a funny name, kind of old-fashioned, you know."

Roy Dale said, "You don't hear it much."

Runt said, "I never liked it much, myself. It was my daddy's name."

Roy Dale said, "Your daddy was named Cyrus?"

Runt said, "I was going to name you Cyrus, that's what your mama wanted to name you, call you Cy."

Roy Dale said, "Well, I'm glad you didn't."

Runt said, "Well, see, that's what I figured. I never cared for the name myself. I figured you wouldn't much like it neither. Sometimes, though, I still kind of wish I had of give you my name. You mought've liked it, if you wont never called nothing else."

Roy Dale said, "I don't think so."

Runt said, "If you'd of been a girl, we was going to name you Janie."

Roy Dale said, "Well, I'm glad I wont a girl."

Runt laughed.

He said, "Well, yeah. Janie was my mama's name."

Roy Dale said, "I had a grandmama name of Janie?"

Runt said, "Well, yeah."

Roy Dale said, "Uh-huh."

Runt said, "Well, think about it."

Roy Dale said, "I got to go to school."

Runt said, "Honey, they was a body found down in Roebuck, out from the spillway."

All of a sudden Roy Dale felt the arrows float up out of the quiver across his shoulder and float out into the air, away from him. He felt the re-curved bow disintegrate into a powder and scatter itself lightly across the floor.

Roy Dale said, "I got to go to school."

Runt said, "Maybe that's why I want to change my name. I don't know."

Roy Dale said, "What time is it?"

Runt said, "You're going to be hearing about it, it's a murder, a terrible murder, I just thought I ought to tell you."

Roy Dale said, "I got to go, I'm own be late."

Runt said, "I love you, son. I don't think I never told you that."

Roy Dale said, "Really, I'm own be late."

ROY DALE didn't have an arrow catcher today. Sweet Austin didn't come to school, and neither did Sugar Mecklin. He figured this out in first period study hall.

He leaned over to Baby Raby, who was about twenty-one years old, she flunked seventh grade so many times, and had large breasts.

He said, "Hey, Baby Raby, you seen Sugar or Sweet?"

Baby Raby said, "Roy Dale Conroy, have you ever washed your feet one day in your en-tire life? I could smell your feet the minute you walked on the school grounds."

Baby Raby wasn't dumb, she was smart. She flunked seventh grade three times out of spite alone.

Roy Dale said, "I washed my feet plenty of times."

Truth was, he couldn't remember the last time he washed his feet, or anything else, and he had to admit, he thought he smelled something a little foul hisself, before Baby Raby ever brought up the subject. Wonder why his aunt Alice didn't mention it to him lately. Alice, look like she's falling down on the job. Look like Coach Heard might of said something.

He turned the other way, to the other side of the aisle. Wesley McNeer was sitting there, he would be. Wesley looked like an ape. His hair grew halfway down his forehead and he walked stooped over and his arms were real long. His mama always packed Wesley a banana in his lunch. Look like Wesley's mama was proud Wesley looked like an ape. Wesley's mama ought to send Wesley to school with a tin cup and an accordion, put a little red hat on his head, just as soon.

Roy Dale said, "Hey, Wesley, you monkey-looking piece of shit."

Wesley said, "Is that your breath or your feet?"

Roy Dale said, "You one of the purple-butted primates."

Wesley said, "Get bent, Gravedigger Junior."

Roy Dale said, "Let's see your tail."

Wesley said, "My tail?—well shoot, where's my tail, I must of done left my tail over to your house when I was fucking your mama, bring it to school with you tomorrow, will you, Roy Dale, leave it in my locker."

Roy Dale and Wesley were giggling their heads off and going *shh, shh, shh*.

Miss Coney was the study hall teacher, plenty mean, eyes like Flash Gordon ray guns. Don't mess with Miss Coney.

Miss Coney said, "Maybe you two boys would like to share the fun with the rest of the study hall."

Some teachers can say that and you know right off that you can mop up the school with their job. Miss Coney says that and you start worrying about what she gone be using for a mop.

Wesley said, "Roy Dale said I look like a monkey, and that hurt my feelings."

Miss Coney was so mean nobody even giggled. Everybody thought Wesley looked like a monkey, even Miss Coney.

What was Roy Dale supposed to say to defend himself?

Should he draw more attention to the fact of his smelly feet?

Roy Dale said, "I said I was sorry. I done already apologized."

Wesley said, "That's true, Miss Coney, he did apologize, and I accepted his apology."

Miss Coney said, "Well, all right, then, let's just leave it at that."

Even Miss Coney couldn't be sharp all the time.

Later on, Roy Dale whispered, "Where's Sweet Austin?"

Wesley said, "He found a dead nigger."

Roy Dale said, "He *what*?"

Wesley said, "They give you a day off from school if you can find a dead nigger. I'm own find me one this afternoon, might see can I find two or three, I been needing a little vacation."

Roy Dale and Wesley giggled, they snorted, they said *shh, shh, shh*, they laughed their durn heads off, they was so tickled.

Miss Coney looked up, but she didn't catch them this time, not a chance, they were too sharp for Miss Coney today.

So that was the way Roy Dale's day started out.

There were all these jokes about the dead nigger, all day long.

The main joke had to do with the gin fan that was found tied around the neck of the body, the hundred-pound engine and propellor that had been fastened to the corpse with a strand of barbed wire.

The joke was that a nigger had tried to steal a gin fan and swim across the lake with it.

Kids were laughing about these jokes all day long.

Roy Dale sure did laugh, whoo boy, Roy Dale got a kick out of all these jokes. What was even better, though, was when he found somebody who hadn't heard one of them, then he could tell the joke his ownself, make somebody else laugh, too. Now that was something. "Stole a gin fan and was trying to swim across the *lake* with it!" he would say.

Everybody was laughing. Roy Dale even made Baby Raby laugh, no telling what she'd be letting him do next.

Other new information crept in, from time to time, during the day. Lord Montberclair and Mr. Gregg had been arrested for murder.

Roy Dale kept on laughing so much he didn't think about Lord Montberclair and Mr. Gregg. He didn't think about his mama coming back home. He didn't even think about the body in Roebuck being the same as the one Runt had told him about, which seemed like it must be a white person, for some reason.

About all Roy Dale thought about was that he wouldn't have an arrow-catching partner at practice this afternoon.

Soon after the last bell of the day, the locker room in the

gym, out behind the schoolhouse, started to fill up with boys, arrow catchers and archers.

Roy Dale looked around, hoping Sweet or Sugar might have come to school late, sometime during the day, after study hall, maybe Coach Heard would let them practice, after all.

Roy Dale's quiver and bow lay in the bow rack of his locker, where he'd stored them first thing this morning after he got to school. He touched each with a secret intimacy, tenderness, and then he rattled them against the boards of the bow rack in a manly, careless way, just in case anybody got the wrong idea.

He sat down on the wooden bench in front of the lockers and started to take off his shoes. The weight-lifting set, barbells and dumbbells and extra iron plates and the wrench, lay in a corner nearby.

A bucktoothed kid name Phillip, the team manager, fussed around the players with an equipment kit, prepping ankles or wrists or rib cages with Tuff-Skin, sticky yellow stuff that he smeared on with a brush to protect the skin from tape burn, and then applying strips of adhesive tape, which he tore off neatly in short, uniform strips.

He changed broken cleats, if need be, he issued new equipment, bowstrings, or arrows, he arranged times with players who wanted analgesic rubdowns after practice.

The concrete floor of the locker room seemed always to be damp and to hold a smell of sweat and smelly feet and dirty socks and unwashed jockey straps, and maybe even urine, from the toilet, which sometimes got stopped up and overflowed. Somebody really ought to mop up this place with Pine-Sol, once in a while.

The shower stall, with its two drizzly spigots and no door or partition, stood just to the right of Roy Dale's locker. Roy Dale knew he ought to take a shower after practice each day, like the other boys—he especially knew it today, because his feet smelled so bad, Baby Raby was right, there was no getting around it—but he was ashamed of the way he looked when he was naked. He had a bad hernia, and one of his balls hung down real low. There was just no privacy, good grief.

The locker room was crowded now, there was a lot of loud talk, some grab-ass and towel-snapping. Boys were naked, or getting out of their street clothes, or putting on the lightweight, loose-fitting practice uniforms for catching or shooting. Some were talking about the new eye-protection that might be required by law, others were talking about girls. Baby Raby's name came up a couple of times, mainly references to her breasts.

Dress-out moved along, same old stuff.

Smoky Viner was there, as always, good Lord, a boy

with a thick neck and a hard head. Nobody could stand Smoky Viner.

Smoky was ramming his head into the wall, like a bull, you never saw anything like it, blammo, the plaster was flying, smack, the doorframe splintered, bong, a metal stanchion rang like a farm bell. You couldn't keep anything nice with Smoky Viner around.

Ramming his head into the wall just tickled the pure-dee shit out of Smoky Viner.

For a while nobody said anything, and then when Smoky didn't stop for a long time, and the smell of plaster dust started to get stronger than the smell of sweat or piss, somebody said, "Smoky, for God's sake, man!"

Smoky Viner was grinning like a billy goat.

Smoky said, "One time I butted down a shithouse, turned it over on its side."

Somebody said, "Well, that's good, Smoky, that's real good, that's something to be proud of."

Everybody hated Smoky Viner.

Smoky Viner said, "They ought to be some kind of butting contest, they ought to be some kind of high school sport for butting."

Somebody said, "Smoky, you gone end up in Whitfield, honest to God, boy."

Smoky butted the stanchion again, bong. He said, "They ought to be some kind of high school sport."

Before long the topic of conversation turned to the dead nigger, it was bound to happen, people had been talking about it, joking about it, anyway, all day long.

The same jokes started up again now, and they were still funny, too, vacation days for finding a dead one, one who stole a gin fan and tried to swim across the lake with it.

Roy Dale was having himself a good time. He was shy to tell a joke in a crowd, so he was quiet, he didn't say much, but he was laughing, boy, oh yes sir.

Then somebody said something that shut the mouth of everybody standing in the locker room. The words froze the smile on Roy Dale's face and caused it to crack and fall right off.

"I'm for the nigger."

That's what somebody said.

Huh? Who said that? What did you say?

On a sudden impulse, Roy Dale turned to Phillip, the bucktoothed boy who was the team's manager.

He said, "Hey, Phillip, you know what we ought to do, we ought to sign us a blood oath together, a pact, you know, like Indians, or pirates, we ought to promise one another, no lie, no smiles, no kidding around, that wherever we end up in life, right here or far away, or when we're young or when we're old, don't matter, that you'll get you some braces to straighten out them buckteeth and I'll get my ball shortened, okay, you want to go in with me on this deal, want to be partners?"

What had got into Roy Dale's head, saying a thing like that!

Phillip looked at Roy Dale like he thought Roy Dale was probably going to end up in Whitfield with Smoky Viner.

Roy Dale said, "Sorry. Just kidding."

Phillip went back to tape and Tuff-Skin.

Except nobody really went back to anything. The words were still in the air.

Did Roy Dale hear those words? He must have.

Everybody shut up. Nobody even noticed what Roy Dale had said to Phillip.

Who said he was for the nigger?

It was Smoky Viner.

Smoky Viner said, "It ain't right."

Maybe it was a dream, that would be one explanation.

It wasn't a dream.

Smoky Viner said, "Y'all ought to be shamed of yourself, laughing about a boy got killed."

Roy Dale thought, Yeah, I better take me a shower today, I think I might better start taking me a shower most every day from now on, feet smelling bad as they do.

The room was still very quiet, no one was moving, or scarcely breathing.

Some time passed like this.

Roy Dale wondered why he hadn't known enough to say what crazy Smoky Viner said. Roy Dale even had a daddy that warned him, and he still didn't know enough. Roy Dale was laughing like a durn hyena, that's all Roy Dale was doing. Roy Dale realized he hated Smoky Viner worse than ever.

Finally, in a low voice, almost a whisper, somebody said, "Uh, Smoky, it was a, you know, white lady. A colored boy and a white lady." This was gently said, a means of assuring that the record was straight.

Smoky Viner said, "It ain't right."

Somebody said, "We ain't said it was right, Smoky. We just kidding around."

Smoky Viner said, "I laughed too, I couldn't help it."

Well.

Smoky Viner said, "I hope I live long enough to forgive myself for that laugh."

Roy Dale thought, Maybe I'll ask Runt about an operation to correct this long ball, the hernia. I don't have to wait until I'm old. Runt might could come up with the money, if I asked him.

Smoky Viner said, "I'm shamed of myself. I want to die, I'm so shamed of myself."

There weren't any more jokes. Everybody was about all dressed-out and ready for practice, anyway.

They gathered up their equipment, they rattled their arrows, they strung their bows, they moved out of the locker room and onto the practice field in ones and twos.

There was one more thing that happened that day that Roy Dale would always remember.

The team was out on the wide, green field. The sun had been out for a few days and was warm on their faces.

Roy Dale said, "Coach Heard, Sweet and Sugar neither one ain't here today."

Coach Heard said, "Well, I heard, you know, I heard about the bad news."

Roy Dale said, "Bad news."

Coach said, "Them finding that floater and all."

Roy Dale said, "I was just, you know, wondering—"

Coach Heard said, "How about I pair you off with Smoky today, Smoky Viner ain't got no regular partner. That's the ticket, it'd do him good, too, you take him up under your wing for a day, build up his confidence maybe, sure would, do him some good."

Nobody wanted to be on a team with Smoky Viner, even on a regular day. Smoky Viner couldn't catch an arrow for shit. On the best day of his life, Smoky Viner couldn't catch an arrow.

Roy Dale said, "You want me to team up with Smoky Viner?"

Coach Heard said, "Well, yeah, Roy Dale, I do, I think

I would like for you to do that today."

Coach Heard said, in a confidential way, "Ease up a little on Smoky Viner, you know, take a little bow off that string, won't you, Roy Dale, he ain't real skilled at this game. He's all tore up today, anyway, you know."

In Roy Dale's hand today the bow was a weightless thing, like air, it was so easy to draw to the limit, full forty pounds.

The arrow, when it flew, was, as he had known it would be, all his rage, his emptiness and loss, outward, outward, forever away from his heart. It was mothers gone off to Kosiesko with strangers, grandparents named Cyrus and Janie, graves to earn a family's daily bread.

To Smoky Viner the arrow seemed to emerge from another world into his own. It came towards him, mysterious, whistling, bustling, lustering invisibility, point and shaft and fletch, sucking up, as it flew, all the available oxygen from the atmosphere and into its hungry, insatiable self.

The atmosphere rarified.

Birds fell from the air.

Cattle toppled over in a field.

Car motors stalled on the highway.

The body of the Bobo-child, dressed in a heavy garment of fish and turtles and violent death, reversed all its decay, and flesh became firm once more, eyes snapped back into sockets and became bright, bones unbroke themselves, feet became swift, laughter erupted like music, and bad manners and disrespect and a possessive disdain for a woman became mere child's play, a normal and decent testing of adolescent limits in a hopeful world.

The arrow hit Smoky Viner in the dead middle of his forehead.

Maybe Roy Dale could learn to call Runt "Daddy," he believed he could try. Maybe he could learn to speak words of love to him, though he felt nothing in his heart like love. Maybe he could speak to his mother honest words of rage for leaving him behind. Maybe he could believe that his vile laughter at the death of a child, like himself, did not eliminate him from human hope, by its villainy.

The arrow that hit Smoky Viner's head was a "blunt." It struck Smoky Viner so hard that the arrow collapsed upon itself, this density of meaning, and splintered a million ways at once, throwing shards of wood and a spray of sawdust around Smoky Viner's head like the muddy, chaotic rings of Saturn.

Smoky Viner saw little of this. Smoky Viner saw only a flock of tiny bluebirds flying around and around his head, cheep-cheep-cheeping some familiar tune, perhaps the lullaby that Dumbo's mother sang to the baby elephant in the cartoon movie Smoky Viner saw one time, he was just not sure, good night, little one, good night.

Everyone else on the field saw only a miracle.

They saw Smoky Viner, for once in his life, still standing but knocked unconscious by a blow to the head.

He teetered, he began to fall.

They saw a boy with courage to speak words that they had not had courage even to think.

They saw hope.

For themselves, for the Delta, for Mississippi, maybe the world.

Coach Heard hollered, "Roy Dale!"

Smoky Viner toppled over, like a tree felled in a forest.

Coach Heard hollered, "Smoky Viner!"

Roy Dale emptied his quiver onto the ground, the seven remaining arrows, and found the steel-tipped arrow among them, the one that he drove into his wall at night.

He separated it from the rest. He held it in both hands in front of him. He broke it across his knee, crack, and flung the two pieces aside.

He said, "I'm sorry, I'm sorry, I'm sorry!"

11

Arrow Catcher began to fill up with strangers.

They seemed to be everywhere. They wore ties, some of them, in this heat. They loosened their ties and opened their shirt collars. They took off their jackets and carried them flung over one shoulder. They took a good look at everything. They looked like people visiting the zoo.

Every time the Greyhound pulled up to the curb in front of the Arrow Cafe, and the bus doors whooshed open, more new strangers got off. Most of them were white men, with suitcases in the compartment beneath the bus. Some carried leather valises off the bus with them. Some even carried small typewriters in hard cases.

They stood on the curbside. They looked around them, right and left.

These were the reporters from *Look* and *The New York Times*, all the papers and magazines from outside the South.

They wiped their faces and necks with white handkerchiefs. They said, "Humid."

They looked at the retired farmers sitting on benches on the square, men in Big Smith overalls and wearing brogans on their feet. Men with sun-creased faces and a pack of Red Man stuck out of a back pocket.

The reporters said, "Amazing."

They looked at the loiterers around the courthouse. They noticed the white men with unshaven chins and crumpled straw hats, standing about the courthouse green. They noticed the coloreds segregating themselves beneath the Confederate statue.

They said, "Do you believe this?"

They noticed the statue of the Confederate soldier in front of the courthouse, with a hand up to his brow to shade the sun.

Somebody said, "That old boy is facing south."

Somebody else said, "He's planning his retreat."

This gave them a laugh. They had a few good, strong male laughs about this. "He's planning his retreat!" they said, many times.

They went into the Arrow Cafe and looked at the menu.

They whispered to one another, "Fried catfish."

They whispered, "Collard greens."

To the girl behind the counter, they said, "Do you have any grits?"

This gave them a good laugh, too. They laughed their heads off about this joke. Grits!

"How about selling us some grits, sweetcheeks," they said.

These boys never had such a good laugh.

The girl said, "Just at breakfast."

She knew they were making fun of her, she just wasn't sure what the joke was all about.

They looked at the trees in a small park in the center of town. They said, "Which one of these trees is a magnolia tree?"

They said, "Are there any alligators around here?"

"Snapping turtles?"

These boys knew how to laugh.

They asked colored men standing on a corner if they would sing a verse or two from "Old Man River." They were serious. They said they'd be willing to pay two dollars just to hear a verse or two of "Old Man River" by an authentic soul of the South.

The colored men said they couldn't recollect ever having heard of that song.

The reporters said, "Amazing."

They wrote dispatches for their newspapers and magazines. They wrote that the scenery itself was hostile. *The scenery is as oppressive as the moss that hangs from the cypress trees*, they wrote. *The silence is like taut skin,* they wrote, *and the faint heart startles, when that silence is cracked by the hiss of a suddenly opened Coke.*

That's the way they wrote about Arrow Catcher, Mississippi. It was pure-dee poetic.

They shook their heads in disbelief at everything they saw.

They said, "Faulkner was only a reporter."

They said, "Faulkner was only the camera's eye."

They went up to men sitting on benches in front of Wooten's Cobbler Shop. They said, "Where is the nearest motel?"

The men on the benches considered the question. They leaned down between their legs and spit into a lard bucket and wiped snuff drippings off their chin.

The men on the benches said, "The nearest whut?"

The out-of-town visitors repeated this story many times. "And so then this old guy spits, you know, down into a pail of some kind, and then he looks up, real thoughtful, you know, and he says—get this, it's going to kill you—he says, 'The nearest *whut*?' " Oh boy, what a joke! " 'The nearest *whut*?' "

So the tourist season had fallen upon Arrow Catcher, Mississippi.

The Arrow Hotel was back in business.

Miss Peabody was back in business.

The old lady who owned the Arrow Hotel, who pronounced her name Miz Pee-buddy, had not been seen or heard from in years. A ghost might as well have been picking up the occasional two dollars from beneath the shot glass beside the register-book, her presence was so scarce.

Now, one morning, Miz Peebuddy showed up on the

front porch sitting in a high-backed rocking chair, as if she had never been gone. She was fanning herself with a church fan and watching all the commotion. She was wearing dollar signs in her eyes.

Miz Peebuddy complained to one reporter that there used to be a sign on the outskirts of town that said ARROW CATCHER A GOOD PLACE TO RAISE A BOY.

She said nobody knew where that sign was anymore, didn't know what went with it. She said it was a shame, too, a crime and a shame to misplace a nice sign like that.

She said the sign had been shot several times from passing cars—she said Big Boy Chisholm, the marshal, had confirmed this fact—and then it was taken down, for some unknown reason, she said, and it had never been replaced.

"Now nobuddy knows where the old sign went, let alone a new one. Just when we need some good publicity around here, all you kind strangers arriving in our little town, we ought to be making our best impression on you, and nobuddy seems to be able to find the sign."

Miz Peebuddy said, "A few bullet holes don't make the message unreadable if the message is strong."

Miz Peebuddy was hot news. Miz Peebuddy made the New York papers two days in a row. Miz Peebuddy hit the AP wires.

Miz Peebuddy didn't care. She didn't notice. There was

a new sign above the register-book at the Arrow Hotel. It replaced the sign that said $2. The new sign, with its own strong message, said $5.

Miz Peebuddy carried a little metal strongbox full of money around with her.

She said, "I hope you boys like biscuits and ham gravy. That's what we're having for breakfast tomorrow."

They looked at one another. When Miz Peebuddy was out of the room, they broke up. They said, "Biscuits and ham gravy! For breakfast!"

New details about one thing and another came out in the newspaper every day—a federal judge was chosen, Durwood Swinger.

The prosecutor was a local boy, a graduate of Arrow Catcher High. He had a deep limp, from a case of polio when he was a child. He gave a little skip to his step when he walked. People who knew him called him Hopalong Cassidy, because of that skip in his step. The paper even reported this.

A New Orleans lawyer was named for the defense. Poindexter Montberclair could afford it. Solon Gregg was flying on Lord Montberclair's coattails.

The two defendants were being tried together, the papers said.

Now that was a surprise, people said. It didn't look like

Lord Montberclair would want his name attached to the
Gregg name in this public way, people said. Even if they
did do the killing together, those people said. White trash
like Gregg and a fine man like Lord Montberclair, well, my
gracious, what won't they think of next.

The two defendants admitted taking the boy out of the
house. The newspapers learned this through their New
Orleans lawyer. Mr. Gregg had been kind enough to report
the infraction in a local hangout, the problem, the breach
of etiquette, the wolf whistle, whatever you want to call it,
and the two together had gone to speak to the boy, the New
Orleans lawyer said.

My clients only meant to scare him, their lawyer told the
reporters. That was reasonable, wasn't it?—after what the
boy said to Lady Montberclair? Whistling like that? But
they sure didn't kill him, the New Orleans lawyer told the
newspapers. They warned him, well sure, they admitted
doing that, but then they let him go, right after they gave
him a good talking-to, a good scare.

They said they told him, "Now you git on back home,
boy, and don't let us never catch you doing such of a thing
again." They said they didn't know what happened to the
boy after that. They figured he walked on back home, like
they told him to. He seemed like an obedient child, so they
just figured he went on home. All they did was scare him.

People talked about this all over the county.

People said, "Well, now, I can see their point there. If all they done was take the boy out and give him a scare, a good strong warning, well, there wont really no harm in that, now was there. That boy needed some sense shook into his head. Wonder where he went after they left him go?"

The out-of-state press reported every word. When Delta people saw their words in print, they were astonished, some of them.

One man had repeated the joke about a nigger trying to swim across Roebuck with a gin fan he had stolen, and then a couple of days later, there it was, his words, printed on the front page of *The New York Times*.

The report made the statement seem as though the man actually believed this to be true, that he believed a colored person had actually done this foolish thing and had drowned as a result of it. And there was his name, his full name, right beside what he had said and supposedly believed!

The reporter who filed the report handed the newspaper to the man at the marble soda fountain in Mr. Shanker's Drug Store.

The man said, "What'd you want to write a thing like that for? That was just a joke."

The reporter said, "It wasn't much of a joke."

The man said, "Well, I grant you that."

The reporter said, "What have you got to say about it?"

The man said, "Well, it looks like to me all this attention you been giving to this little town is about as bad as a durn nigger murder."

And then the next day, this statement appeared in the newspaper as well, and again the man's name was right beside it. DELTA MAN SAYS REPORTING TRUTH THE SAME AS MURDER.

There came a hunkering down, a defensiveness.

Bumper stickers started to appear around the Delta.

They said, MISSISSIPPI—THE MOST LIED ABOUT STATE IN THE UNION.

They said, BOBO'S BLOOD IS ON THE HANDS OF THE SUPREME COURT.

The Supreme Court became the villain. The *Brown v. Board of Education* decision.

The local press latched onto this idea.

The *Greenwood Commonwealth* reporter wrote, "For the Negro vote in such places as Harlem, these Men of Expediency on the Court have been willing to put into serious jeopardy the peace of the Southland."

This particular reporter seemed to think Supreme Court judges were elected. It didn't matter. Mississippi was on dee-fence.

Jars with March of Dimes messages on them were taken

down from shelves and dusted off and printed with the words DEFENSE FUND and set out on counters of stores to collect money to help pay the New Orleans lawyer.

Not much money was collected, considering Lord Montberclair was one of the richest men in the Delta, but some was, a few quarters and dollar bills showed up in the jars, as a means of protesting all the outside interference, all the agitation.

During jury selection, Uncle and Auntee went into hiding.

The young prosecutor, the boy with a limp, said, "Uncle, put your grief aside and find yourself a hiding place. We need you alive for this trial."

OUTSIDE, ON the courthouse steps, a child asked his daddy, "How come they let Mr. Runt bring his parrot to the courthouse?"

His daddy said, "You delving into some areas where I ain't got much expertise, punkin."

The child said, "How can it be a hunnert percent humidity and it don't be raining?"

His daddy said, "Well—"

The child said, "Who would win in a fight between Jesus Christ and Superman?"

His daddy said, "Jesus Christ would kick Superman's steel ass, and don't you forget it, podner."

The child said, "Are they gone electrocute these murderers?"

His daddy said, "Naw, honey, they probably ain't, although they richly deserve it."

The child said, "How come Charlie McCarthy's buddy is called Mortimer Snerd?"

His daddy said, "Everybody's got to be called something."

The child said, "How come Mr. Runt's gone change his name?"

His daddy said, "I'm gone start calling you Mortimer Snerd, what I'm own do. Call you Snerd for short."

The child said, "What's that expression mean when you say somebody is ugly as hammered shit?"

His daddy said, "Well—"

The child said, "What's a turd tapper?"

His daddy said, "You the onliest turd tapper I know about, you little turd tapper."

The child said, "What's that expression mean when you say somebody's breath is so bad it can back shit up a hill?"

His daddy said, "I'd say that one's more or less self-explanatory."

The child said, "How come Mr. Runt don't call hisself Digger O'Delve, like on Life of Riley?"

His daddy said, "O'Delve is an Irish name, Runt comes from Scotch-Irish descent, seem like I remember. I think that would be the main reason for not choosing Digger O'Delve."

The child said, "What would it feel like to murder somebody?"

His daddy said, "Let's go over to Mr. Shanker's and get us a cone of cream, hell with this durn trial."

The child said, "Do you think we'll ever escape?"

His daddy said, "Not me, punkin, it's too late for me. Maybe you."

The child said, "When you die, what happens?"

His daddy said, "I don't know, sweetnin. Maybe Jesus holds you in his arms and tells you a story about Effie and Peffie."

The child said, "What would be the meaning of the expression where you say somebody went under the limbo stick?"

His daddy said, "Where did you hear about a limbo stick?"

The child said, "I don't remember."

His daddy said, "It mought have something to do with the expression when you say somebody looks like he got beat with an ugly stick, do you reckon?"

The child said, "I own know. Maybe."

His daddy said, "Yew own know, maybe. Come on, how about a cone of Mr. Shanker's cream?"

The child said, "When you die and get buried in Miss-sippi, are you still, you know, *in* Miss-sippi?"

His daddy said, "Naw, honey. That's the whole point about magic. God is good, it don't matter how it looks on the surface of things."

12

THE COURTROOM was jam-pack full of people, and the temperature was up in the nineties, maybe more, so it was plenty hot, too, hot as blue blazes, if you asked Alice Conroy, and the humidity! The courtroom looked like a can of sour-deens, that's what Alice thought about it, and didn't smell no better, if Alice was any judge.

Alice Conroy had never in her life seen so many people jammed up in one place, up underneath one roof.

When Uncle and Auntee were brought into the courtroom they were walking behind Hopalong Cassidy, the prosecutor, his funny little skip-step. Step-and-a-hitch-step, step-and-a-hitch-step. That's the way Hopalong Cassidy, the prosecutor, walked.

Alice could see the two of them, Uncle and Auntee, right down on top of their old heads, from where she sat, up in the balcony, along with the fourth grade and the colored people. The two old folks walked in behind the prosecutor Hopalong Cassidy, stepping and hitch-stepping right along with him, trying to keep up.

Alice's field trip, the fourth-graders, who now had visited every conceivable point of interest in Arrow Catcher, Mississippi, including the sewage treatment pond where they rode around in a motor launch on a sea of human waste, and the Indian mound where they dug up stone-age pots and arrowheads, and the Prince of Darkness Funeral Parlor where they looked at a body, had been assigned the front row of the courtroom balcony. Everybody else up in the balcony, besides themselves, was colored.

Well, Alice couldn't help that. She was sorry if the coloreds were offended by their presence, honest to goodness she was, and she understood well enough what kind of boundary was being crossed here, and she was also just as sorry as she could be if she was taking up seats that other colored people might have sat in, since the courtroom was segregated and there might well be a ton of black folks with just as much right as a bunch of lily-white, thumb-sucking, hair-twisting, pants-peeing fourth graders to be watching the turning of the wheels of justice, such as they were in the sorriest state in the nation, but that was just too bad, too, because she wasn't giving up the seats she had fought so hard to get for her fourth graders, not a chance, even if a field trip to a murder trial might be hard for some educators more experienced and knowledgeable than herself to justify.

Alice had warned her fourth graders before they ever left the schoolhouse not to be laughing at Mr. Hopalong's way of walking, it was a handicap, an affliction, and not a blessed thing he could do about it or don't you think he would, and everybody ought to be grateful they didn't have polio, so take their polio naps and don't swim in Roebuck Lake until they find a cure, was Alice Conroy's best advice.

Alice watched Uncle look around him and see only white-folks. White, Lord, Lord, all that white. Alice could tell that Uncle thought that only white people had been allowed to come to the court. That's got to be a lonely feeling, it seemed like to Alice—especially if you figure most of the whitefolks in question would just love to see Uncle dead for coming here to testify against a white man in the first place, and probably carrying guns to prove it, if anybody in charge of this circus had brain one or thought to check anybody's pants pocket.

All those white people down there! White! Even to Alice it looked like an abomination of some kind. White, white, bird dooky, white, it was sickening, a pestilence!

Alice thought about the Ancient Mariner, water water everywhere, and none of it doing him one bit of good. She thought that's what Uncle must be feeling right about now, because she was feeling it, too, whitefolks whitefolks everywhere, and every durn one of them bitter as bile as the day is long.

She thought about Ahab and the whiteness of the Great Whale, the eternal evil verity of its metaphorical and blub-bery self, as Dr. Dust would say, just like old lardass Hot

McGee, sitting down there with his big fat lazy butt drap-
ing off all sides of the straight-back chair he'd pulled out
in the aisle to sit in because his rear end was too big to sit
on one of the regular benches. Hot McGee always carried
his own chair with him, and a bullwhip, too, wherever he
went, and looked a little bit like a lion tamer except he was
so fat.

Alice thought Uncle was Captain Ahab, even though
Uncle never asked for his troubles or went looking for them
either one, like Ahab did, and Hot McGee, with his fore-
arms like hamburger meat, was the great white whale itself,
and the whale in its ancient stupidity and carelessness had
made its turn back towards the *Pequod*, coming after you,
Ahab, watch out. Every seat, every bench in the courtroom
was full.

Alice saw Uncle look at his unfriendly surroundings. All
white people. Everywhere. White. Uncle looked right and
he looked left. White, white, all white, nothing but white,
so help me God. Alice wanted to call out to him: *Up here!
The colored people are up here, we're up here, above you!* Of
course Alice was white herself, and not colored—nothing's
simple.

Uncle hadn't heard anything, of course.

Then all those white faces looked at Uncle.

All that anger, all that white hatred, rage, a still, sweating, stinking, brooding, engorged buildingful of it, absences large enough, solid enough, to build furniture upon. Uncle could feel it. Uncle thought he was dead meat. He thought he was about to join his nephew in the Promised Land on The Other Side. Alice knew this, because she could feel it, too. All that white and miserable hatred, as ancient and impersonal as geology and fear.

Alice hated the whiteness of her own skin, she ached in her heart for the white children sitting along the balcony rail with her, with their dear name tags fastened to a washed-out shirt or a limp cotton print dress, the whiteness whose history they had never asked to participate in, to be infected by, whose racial genes they shared with Shakespeare, and with men in sheets holding crosses engulfed in flames. The whiteness hit Uncle the same way it hit Alice, like a deafening noise, as elemental as oceanic geography, glacial, straight in the face.

Uncle turned to Auntee, as they moved slowly down the aisle, hippity-hop, hitch-stepping in rhythm with the prosecutor, among the great, ancient watery walls of the Redneck Sea of scowling whites held back on either side by Moses' staff, or God's love, or some magic in the hitch-step-hip-hop of the local boy with polio, Hopalong Cassidy of Arrow Catcher, Mississippi.

Uncle leaned towards her, said something to her, to his wife, Alice could not hear what, of course, but she could imagine. She imagined that the old man said, "Auntee, honey, I'se a dead man."

Auntee held onto his arm. They were Columbus's ship, tempest-tossed and steady as she goes on a stormy sea.

It had not been easy for Alice to get these good spectator seats, along the balcony rail, or any seat in this courthouse at all, let alone sixteen seats together for as many days as she wanted them. Or to get permission to bring fifteen nine-year-olds to a murder trial, though she had broken the ground with the field trip into Balance Due, and another to have the children motored through liquid shit at the sewage reservoir in the farming community of Good Dog Bad Dog, and another to watch an embalming at the Prince of Darkness funeral parlor, though that excursion had been cancelled at the last minute and the class had had to settle for seeing a couple of already-prepared corpses and a lecture on modern embalming techniques and ethical guidelines, one of which was not to allow civilians to watch the process, no matter the educational value, though there was nothing illegal about inviting guests.

Alice was not certain, in fact, how their being here in this courtroom had been accomplished, though she knew that without Mr. Archer's intercession with Judge Swinger, nothing would have been possible. It embarrassed Alice to remember the clear evidence of heartache in the vice principal when she asked Mr. Archer for his permission to take the class to the trial, the pain of his longing and love (it must have been love, mustn't it, to drive him so far beyond job safety for himself and conventional educational practice and even common sense, for there was no telling how much emotional damage Alice was actually doing to these innocent children) and hopeless certainty that he, Mr. Archer, had been placed upon earth to serve and adore this woman who did not love him, and him already married and got four children anyhow, adorable children.

It made Alice wish that it was in her power to love him, to give over in sacrifice to him her body and soul, as she had done to Dr. Dust, though she was aware that because she could not, Mrs. Archer ended up with a better deal than Mrs. Dust, and so that was something to be grateful for, Alice supposed, and she couldn't have done it in any case. She had already loved one married man too many.

Alice kept looking down into the courtroom. The press table for white people was up in the front of the courtroom, under the bench. The colored press table was smaller, a card table, squeezed over to one side of the room, almost out of sight of the bench. At last Uncle looked in the direction of the colored press table. Alice saw Uncle see a few colored faces. She saw the sight of blackness change him for the better. The old man's body seemed to grow stronger, just in that second.

Maybe it was Alice's will, her great need to protect him, if only by magic, that caused Uncle then, for no good reason, to turn suddenly, and to look back up behind him into the balcony.

"Yes!" Alice called out suddenly, without knowing that she was about to speak at all. "We are here! We colored people are behind you!"

Every white face on the main floor of the courtroom turned to stare at Alice. Every dark face as well, from down below, those few, and the hundred or so in the seats around her and behind her. They looked at Alice as if she had just escaped from the lunatic asylum at Whitfield. She might as well have been a witch in Salem.

None of this bothered Alice at all. She waved her arm broadly so that Uncle might see her, the one person on earth she cared whether saw her. She waved her arms, back and forth like a semaphore, as if from a desert island to a ship at sea, Robinson Crusoe, the Swiss Family Robinson, Long John Silver, to their rescuers, or from ship to shore, or to other ships, the Ancient Mariner in still seas beckoning the flagship of the dead, or some doomed sailor waving from the crow's nest of the *Pequod*. *Land Ho!*—or *Thar she blows!*—or some other relevance so large, to Alice anyway, that its significant hold upon her heart could only be contained in metaphors as large as oceans, in loss and isolation as great as creaking sea-borne vessels and windless rigging, canvas and line, buoyed upon salt seas, narrow coffins, watery graves.

Alice's fourth graders waved, too. *Hello, hello, old colored man in pain, old pained colored woman by his side, little polio dancer in front like Jack in the Beanstalk saying to the Giant, I hitch my hatchet and down I go, I hitch my hatchet and down I go, hello all you spectators at the circus, we are here, we are waving our arms as our teacher waves hers, we are saying in loud voices that we are colored people when we know we are not, we are wearing our name tags though we have forgotten our names or any innocence out of which name tags are originally born, denied our heritage for reasons unclear, we are suffering damage from this field trip into the heart of darkness and from our teacher that we may never recover from and we don't care because we love her and become visible to ourselves in her presence, and for reasons obscure we love you, too, old colored man, old colored woman, grieving souls, we suffer your loss, we fear for your life, we don't know what is going on at all.*

Well, that was all right. Didn't make no difference to Uncle where they sat, the other colored people. Didn't make no difference to Uncle if some of them was white, and only children. Uncle was relieved to see them at all. Uncle never had realized just how important it was to have a few colored people around. You'd think that sort of thing would be obvious, wouldn't you, and not just to a colored man, because Alice was thinking the same thing, just as Uncle entertained the thought, and the spiritual relief and redemption that suddenly the thought afforded all who cared or dared to think it.

A white man in the audience said, "Look! Look at the old man! He's checking the house for niggers."

The white man's wife looked up at Alice, waving from the balcony, buttressed by a bank of dark faces who looked ready to blame Alice if anybody else got killed.

Timid, the white man's wife raised her little white hand, not much, just above her waist, halfway to her chest, no more than that, and she waved a shy wave, using only the tips of her fingers, up in the direction of Alice, who seemed even to this white woman, who lived with a greater fear of metaphor than of colored people, to be standing upon, signaling from, the deck of a ship surging on high and northern seas. No one saw her wave, of course, not her husband, and least of all Alice.

The white man said to his wife, "Ninety-five percent of them's not even ours. Our niggers is out picking cotton and tending to they own bidness."

Hey, Alice, the white woman said, or breathed, or imagined, or prayed, since there were no words, no sound, but only a rare and magical identification with the universe and all its suns and foreign stars whose galaxies were visible only from some warm spot near her heart. *I see you, Alice, I see the children with you.* Nothing more, nothing from which meaning might have been extrapolated, but it was enough. *I see you, Alice.*

The man said, "All the dressed-up niggers is strangers. See that?"

The man's wife said, "I see."

Alice watched Hopalong Cassidy whisper to Uncle. She imagined that he told Uncle of the guns hidden in boots and pockets and shoulder holsters in this audience. She imagined that he told Uncle what was obvious, that he could be murdered today, himself, for his testimony.

Uncle whispered some reply, who knows what.

Alice imagined that he whispered, "Much obliged for reminding me."

The sergeant-at-arms was a boy in his early twenties named Peter Skeeter. He was half Choctaw Indian and didn't want to lose this job. He was wearing the uniform of the former sergeant-at-arms, who had been much larger, and so his uniform was baggy and his cap came down over his ears. He kept pushing the cap's bill up out of his eyes. He had made his way to the balcony now.

He said, "Miss Alice, scuse me."

Alice knew the boy because he had a little brother in fourth grade, Jeeter Skeeter.

Alice said, "Hey, Peter Skeeter."

He said, "Judge Swinger, you know—"

She said, "I got a little carried away."

He said, "I ain't trying to be uppity."

She said, "I know, Peter Skeeter." Alice sat down in her seat and promised to behave herself.

Jeeter Skeeter, the little boy, Peter Skeeter's brother, who was sitting down the row, said, "Hey, Peter Skeeter."

He said, "Hey, Jeeter Skeeter." He said, "How come you was saying just now that you's a colored person?"

Jeeter Skeeter said, "I *am* a colored person."

Peter Skeeter said, "Well, not in the usual sense of the word."

He was deferential and sweet, and he understood that this was not an issue to be settled easily, or right this minute.

At the front of the courtroom, Uncle helped Auntee get seated in her chair at the table, and then he went around and dragged out a chair for himself and sat down like he didn't sleep too good last night and he was tired.

Sheriff Trippett came in. Alice recognized him, he was a huge man, with a big pearl-handled pistol on his hip and a white Stetson hat on his head. He was one of the witnesses who would testify later, the High Sheriff.

The sheriff was smiling and glad-handing whoever was in reach. He spoke in a noisy, friendly way to everyone. You could hear him all the way up in the balcony.

"Dexter," he said to one defendant, hitching up his

gunbelt. His big voice drew everybody's attention like a bass drum.

Alice said to her class, "That's the High Sheriff."

Alice's class said, "Oooo!"

"Solon," the sheriff said to the other defendant. Big voice, all over the courtroom, all over town, seemed like, whenever he spoke.

Little Jeeter Skeeter said, "Don't make us ride in no motorboat, Miss Alice." Jeeter Skeeter never had gotten over the boat ride across the sewage reservoir, and he was having a hard time keeping his mind on his business.

Alice said, "Hush up, Jeeter Skeeter, I love you and won't let any harm come to you."

To the New Orleans lawyer, the sheriff said, "Hey, now, Nawlins lawyer! Pleased to meet you!"

A little girl who never stopped twisting her hair said to Alice, "Is they gone be any more dead bodies to look at?"

Well, Alice just had to admit, not every field trip was a complete and unqualified success. The Prince of Darkness Funeral Parlor might just fall into that category.

To the prosecutor, the sheriff said, "Hey there, Hopalong!"

To the white press table, he waved a big wide-fingered hand. He said, "Hello, New Yawk reporters!"

To the reporters at the black press table, he said, "Mawnin', niggers!"

Sheriff Trippett was in a fine, fine mood this morning, that he was, yessir, a high mood. He found himself a good place to sit. Whoa! Whew! Take a load off, Annie!

To Hot McGee he said, "Hey, Lardass!"

He stretched out his long legs and got comfortable, yes he did. Oh yes, Sheriff Trippett was ready, sho was, ready for the show to begin, let's see us some jugglers, let's see us some high wire, let's see some clowns and dancing bears.

So far Sheriff Trippett was the star of the show. Men waved at him, tried to catch his eye, laughed a little too loud at his antics, elbowed their demure wives and said, "Look, lookee, there, what a man!" and though the High Sheriff was as big as a walrus and smelled like a fried-chicken shack, many of those true wives harbored secret thoughts of themselves in a private place with this armed gentleman, and dangerous dreams.

Things moved along. Alice couldn't keep from enjoying herself. She had a wonderful seat, just behind the balcony rail, she could see everything. She saw Uncle Runt, directly below her, enter the courtroom with his parrot on his shoulder. Peter Skeeter had to tell Runt he couldn't bring no parrot into a court of law.

Alice saw them talking together, and she could hear some of what they said, and could imagine the rest. In fact, some of it she had said herself, the day before, when Runt told her he was taking the bird to the trial.

Peter Skeeter said, "Birds ain't allowed."

Runt said, "Peter Skeeter, this parrot ain't never hurt nobody, and got better sense than most of the people you see sitting in this courtroom."

Peter Skeeter pushed his hat up off his ears. He said, "I'm sorry, Mr. Runt, I truly am, but it ain't allowed."

Runt said, "Fortunata's got allergies, my wife. I try to take the parrot out of the house whenever I can."

Peter Skeeter said, "If it was a seeing-eye dog, now that'd be a different story."

Runt said, "It can't speak a word, so it ain't like it's going to be interrupting testimony."

Peter Skeeter said, "Your parrot cain't talk?"

Runt said, "Not a word."

Peter Skeeter said, "I don't know, Mr. Runt. It ain't allowed, is all I know to tell you. It seems like a real well-behaved parrot to me, so it ain't nothing personal against this particular parrot."

Judge Swinger came into the room, wearing shirtsleeves. Everybody stood up. He sat down and fooled with some papers in front of him, and so then everybody else sat down, too.

In a minute the judge looked up. He said, "Peter Skeeter, git that durn parrot out of this-here courtroom."

Peter Skeeter said, "He cain't talk."

The judge was occupied with his papers, so he looked back down at the desk in front of him and didn't answer.

Runt slid into an empty seat and put the parrot down in his lap, pretty much out of sight.

Peter Skeeter said, "If you was blind and needed the parrot to walk across the street with you, well, like I say, that'd be different."

Runt said, "Just today, Peter Skeeter. Tomorrow I'll leave him at home. Fortunata's got allergies."

Peter Skeeter said, "It'd be kind of funny, though, wouldn't it, a blind man walking behind a parrot."

Peter Skeeter was a little bit of a mess, tell you the truth.

Runt said, "You'd have to walk kind of slow."

Peter Skeeter said, "You'd have to have a long leash."

Runt said, "You would, wouldn't you."

Runt and Peter Skeeter had them a pretty good laugh, but they tried to keep it quiet so Judge Swinger wouldn't get mad at them.

Peter Skeeter said, "The parrot would all-time be hollering at you, 'Watch your step!'"

Runt said, "You are a sight in this world, Peter Skeeter."

Peter Skeeter said, "Blind children could go out for the arrow-catching team, if they had a seeing-eye parrot. 'Arrow! Look out!'"

Runt said, "You bout crazy, Peter Skeeter, that's what

you are. You bout as crazy as your old Choctaw name, you know that? Whoever heard of somebody name of Peter Skeeter?"

Peter Skeeter said, "That parrot'd be hollering, 'Goddamn, somebody done shot an arrow at us!' "

Runt said, "Calm down, Peter Skeeter, you gone get me thrown out of here."

Peter Skeeter said, "Parrot'd be hollering, 'Duck!' "

Peter Skeeter forgot all about it being against the rules to hold a parrot in your lap in a court of law. In a minute he wandered off and found somebody else to talk to, and left Runt alone by himself.

Bailiffs carried pitchers of ice water to the various tables, even the colored press table. Alice told the children to be thinking about pictures they might want to draw to illustrate their field trip to the murder trial. She wanted to keep this day on the educational level, unlike the shit pond, which was more just for fun.

People brought church fans with them and were fanning their brains out. On one side the fans showed Jesus with a lamb sitting up in his lap, might as well have been a housecat, and this made Alice think about Uncle Runt with a parrot on his lap and then this brought a tear up in her throat because she loved her uncle so much and believed he was a little bit like Jesus, if he'd had more opportunities in life. On other fans Jesus was suffering the little children to come onto him, which made Alice think of herself, with all these innocent children around her and all, even if she didn't feel very much like Jesus, since she had excellent reason to believe that Jesus never would in one million years have slept with a married man. And there were even pictures of Jesus on the Cross with some thorns and the water and the Blood, which made Alice think of the little boy who'd got murdered, and this broke poor Alice's heart and made her believe that forevermore she would love the weak and draw them into her heart.

On the other side of the fans were messages about Kamp's Low Price Store, where Mr. Kamp was all time telling somebody's mama, "She'll grow into it!" and the Western Auto, where Mr. Marlin sold roller skates that wouldn't stay on your feet, and the Prince of Darkness Mortuary, which Alice would just as soon forget about.

Before Alice knew it, Uncle had got sworn in.

She said to the children, "Look, look, it's starting, hush up!"

The man with the Bible said, "Do you swear—"

Uncle said, "Yassuh, sho do."

Hopalong Cassidy moved up to the witness box with as little skipping as he could manage.

Hopalong said, "How-do, Uncle."

Uncle said, "Tolerable."

The prosecutor said, "Let's get right down to business, Uncle. We know who you are, you already done told us that, and we know where you live, in a cabin on section four of Runnymede, and we know you live alone with your wife and we know what her name is, and that you're sixty-four years old, all that sound about right to you, Uncle?"

Uncle said, "That's right."

Alice looked down upon her Uncle Runt. The parrot seemed to have gone to sleep.

She looked also at Lady Montberclair, in a chair on the other side of the courtroom—Sally Anne—her golden hair, like a princess. Alice ached to know her, to speak to her, to ask her what it was like to fall in love with a man who betrayed himself and everyone else, what it was like to have had sexual congress with a murderer.

In another chair below her, she saw Mrs. Gregg, Glenn's mama, the little stick-figure, pipe-cleaner woman, tiny as a witch. She whispered to the children. "Look who I see."

The children leaned out over the rail and saw the woman who had changed their lives. In the sweltering heat they hummed quiet verses of the songs of Christmas, just at the sight of her. *Right down Santa Claus Lane.*

The wives of two murderers.

And then the mother of the murdered boy. Alice saw

her as well. She sat in a chair that looked like it had been placed there as an afterthought, behind the prosecution's table. Alice had never seen a colored woman wearing such nice clothes, a dark straight skirt and silk blouse and a light seersucker jacket. Maybe it was true that life was better outside the South. Maybe, somehow, the world really was a place of hope and light, if only the geography were different from what Alice knew about. Well, it couldn't be any worse.

The prosecutor said, "All right, then. Now, please describe, as well as you can, what transpired on the night in question, the night of August 28."

Uncle said, "We's already sleeping, me and Miss Auntee. Bobo, he's sleeping, too."

The prosecutor said, "Bobo was your grand-nephew, am I right?"

Uncle said, "That's right."

The prosecutor said, "And Bobo resided with his mother in Chicago, Illinois, is that right?"

Uncle said, "That's right."

The prosecutor said, "Go on, please."

Uncle said, "I heerd this car, sound like. Just rolling. Didn't have no lights on, motor neither one. Funny-looking little car, look like a pickup truck.

"Two white mens come to the house, one stay out in the

car, other one up on the porch. One on the porch, he had him a big pistol. He banged on the door frame with the butt, you know.

"Me and Miss Auntee, we's already awake now, already done got dressed.

"Man with the pistol, he axe for the boy from Chicago, that's how he called him. He say, 'Whereabouts is the boy from Chicago? Where the one what did the talking at Arrow Catcher?'"

The prosecutor said, "What happened next?"

Uncle said, "Bobo, he come out the back bedroom. Man say, 'Git yo-self dressed,' so he put on some pants, Bobo did. Man say, 'Go git in the car.'"

The prosecutor said, "Only one white man came in the house, the other stayed out in the car, is that correct?"

Uncle said, "That's right."

The prosecutor said, "What happened next?"

Uncle said, "Man hit Bobo upside the head. Hit him with the butt end of his pistol, laid open a gash in his face, too."

Up in the balcony, Alice looked along the row to see whether the children were all right. There was a lot of pants-wetting and crying at the funeral parlor, and probably permanent emotional damage, too, if Alice was willing to admit it. It didn't take much to send a field trip straight out of control.

The prosecutor said, "All right."

Uncle said, "Man pushed Bobo out the door, out to the little car."

The prosecutor said, "The little car that looked like a pickup truck."

Uncle said, "That's right."

The prosecutor said, "Was there someone sitting in the truck?"

Uncle said, "That's right."

Alice whispered in a loud, educational voice: "Can anyone tell me who was in the truck?"

A thumbsucker took his hand out of his mouth and said, "I own know."

Alice whispered, "Keep watching."

The prosecutor said, "What happened next?"

Uncle said, "The man in the car hit Bobo in the face with his fist. They was talking, I couldn't hear what they was talking about."

The prosecutor said, "But you could see, couldn't you? You could clearly see what was happening?"

Alice whispered, "Anybody else want to guess?"

A little girl with John the Conqueroo, a voodoo charm made of spices in a felt bag around her neck, said, "Mr. Dexter?"

Alice said, "Excellent! Yes, very good!"

Uncle said, "That's right."

The prosecutor said, "How well could you see this happening? Wasn't it dark?"

Uncle said, "I could see. Light come on in the ceiling of the little car."

The prosecutor said, "So you could see clearly the faces of both men who came to your house in that car that night?"

Uncle said, "That's right."

The prosecutor said, "All right, then, Uncle, I want you to do something for me. I want you to tell me something." He said, "Will you please tell this court whether your own life has been threatened since the day of these events?"

Uncle said, "Sho has."

Alice leaned first one way and then the other, down the line of children. She said, "Is everybody understanding this?"

One child said, "The misuse of power is the root of all evil?"

Alice said, "Well—"

Another child said, "There is no justice on the earth?"

Alice said, "Well—"

Another child said, "We are all alone in the world?"

Alice said, "Well—"

Another child said, "The greatest depth of our loss is the beginning of true freedom?"

Alice said, "Well—"

Another child said, "The disposal of human waste is the responsibility of the brokenhearted?"

These were all phrases Alice had put on the chalkboard after other field trips. It occurred to Alice, hearing these phrases now, that she might have attempted to do too much with a class of fourth graders. She was willing to admit to some excesses.

Alice said, "Just listen."

The prosecutor said, "How often would you say your life has been threatened since then?"

Uncle said, "Most every day, I spect."

The prosecutor said, "Are you afraid to testify here today, Uncle?"

Uncle said, "Sho is."

He said, "Are you afraid for your life?"

Uncle said, "That's right."

He said, "And can you identify those white men who abducted your nephew that dark night?"

Uncle said, "That's right."

Alice's eye fell once more upon her Uncle Runt, with the parrot in his lap.

The prosecutor said, "All right, one more thing before you do. Would you please tell the court whether you have ever pointed your finger in the face of a white man. Have you ever done such a thing before?"

The parrot seemed to have waked up. It shook its head in a delicate little way, and opened its eyes, and looked first one way and then the other.

Uncle looked like a little boy in the witness chair, he was so scared.

He said, "Naw-suh, never pointed my finger in a white man's face."

Runt stroked the parrot's head with his finger.

The prosecutor said, "Well, then, right here in this courtroom full of white people who hate you just for being here—and some of them are carrying guns on them, right this minute—"

The New Orleans lawyer said, "Your honor, honestly!"

Judge Swinger said, "Just ask your question, Mr. Prosecutor."

The prosecutor said, "Can you, for the court, please point out the man who entered your house and then pistol-whipped your nephew and pushed him out the door to the car?"

There was no warning at all for what happened next, none at all, the parrot's leaving Runt's lap and becoming airborne.

Solon Gregg only sat impassively at the defense table, in a chair pulled slightly away from the chairs of the better-dressed gentlemen for the defense, waiting to be pointed at, and wondering how better to threaten with death the man being asked to point him out.

Auntee only wondered which direction the gunshot would come from.

And so the parrot rose up, without prelude or pretext or announcement.

Uncle was wearing clean overalls and a clean shirt. In this strange moment in his life, in which he was being asked for the first time ever to point into the face of a white man, he lifted his right arm as if it were a heavy weight.

The parrot ascended from Runt's lap as if by magic, straight up into the air, the atmosphere, the great interior above-water sea of humidity and disappointed lives. Up and up and up, high up into the high-ceilinged room of the courthouse, as if the room were the wide, endless, hopeful, and magical canopy of the African sky.

Later, trying to recall the details of the parrot's takeoff, Runt would say that he did not even remember the bird's fine claws, strong as a bobcat, releasing from the fabric of his gabardine pants. He would say that he did not remember at all the brush of wing feathers against his face, as there must have been when the bird gathered up enough air beneath its wings to lift off, as if the first several feet of the parrot's upward flight had nothing at all to do with aerodynamics or hollow, pneumatic bones, or wingspan, or

wing-shape, or muscle and sinew and hot blood, or anything at all that could launch so heavy and earth-bound and
satisfied and silent a creature as this feathered beast, not
even a good strong jump or push-off.

One second the parrot was sitting there, content as a
well-fed cat, actually purring, and the next, in the tropical humidity and other-worldly heat of this room with the
same climate as an Amazon rainforest, it was rising in a
straight line as if through liquid, like a porpoise torpedoing
its way upward through blue bubbles from the sandy floor
of the Gulf of Mexico into another atmosphere, another
world, new life.

Perhaps only Uncle, preoccupied with grief and the
probable imminence of his own sudden death, failed to
notice the wild and magical ascent of the African parrot,
generations closer to their shared homeland than Uncle
himself, brother to bright plumage and courageous heart.
He was lifting his weighted arm, the hand, on the end of
it, which would do the pointing, like an anvil.

All other eyes were on the bird, Alice's eyes among them,
the children's eyes, the Judge, who was pounding his gavel,
"Order, order!" Solon Gregg, the murderer who knew nothing of magic or of metaphor, the great, green bird, with
white feet and a red tail, that now, without apparently
a single wingbeat, had attained the fullest height of the
courtroom, above the great windows, and had begun in

earnest to fly, and now at last using its wings, and feathers, and all the other instruments of natural and normal flight.

The parrot was large and it flew, as it must, with deep strokes, but now it flew, or seemed to, anyway, as if it were far, far larger than its actual size. It flew with enormity and ponderousness and sadness and strength, it flew with the deep, slow wingstrokes of a condor, an albatross, oh deep, deep, deep the piston plunges of those sad wings, long the distances that each stroke took the bright bird along its circular course around the courtroom.

High up in the balcony, Alice and her wide-eyed children and the embankment of dark faces saw the parrot best, the strange shape, the layers of feathers, close up, the amazed eyes, the massive open beak and prehensile tongue, the dear, white, and yoke-toed feet, the green plumage and red tail, the underwater quality of its slow-motion flight.

Alice did not travel in this magic moment, as the ebony-colored women and men around her may have done, to dark Africa, Kilimanjaro, and the Ivory Coast, and sorcerers dancing with poison cobras to ensure rainfall, as birds and monkeys chattered and jabbered from the jungle trees.

Alice traveled to her childhood in the swamp, in winter, at night, before her father died, where always, though it was Mississippi, there seemed to Alice to be snow, and always gray footprints, and smoke from the crumbling chimneys of the Negroes' cabins and a song of trains and farm dogs through the still, cold air and the black pine trees, and her father's face a bright mask in the light of the big moon.

These were the days when her father took her owling, when she stood beside his leg and he lifted his mittens to his mouth and called, "Whoo, whoo," and sometimes an echo threaded its way back through the trees, and the echo, her father told her, was the voice of the Great Horned Owl, answering—these were her father's words—"blood with hot blood."

The parrot kept on flying, in its wide circle around the courtroom, and Alice remembered a time when her father had told her, "Call him," meaning the owl, and she had said, "Me?" and he said, "Nobody else," and little Alice, when she was that child in the wilderness with the only man she had ever really loved, put her own hands up, no mittens, and from her throat released into the moony fragrance of the Mississippi darkness and a hunter's moon, a voice she had not known was inside her, a sound of *Whoo, whoo*, which for the first time in all these years came back to her now like a spirit, like justice and freedom, and she had said to her father in that moment, "My breath warmed my hands just now," and her father had said, "You got to make your own heat, sweetness, always, always."

The great exotic bird, the parrot, went on flying, once around the courtroom, twice around the courtroom, faces turned, necks craning to see. Alice heard the bird in near-silent, buoyant flight. It hissed like a cat. It clicked with its bill. Its pneumatic bones creaked with strange joy.

Alice thought of the owl that she called up that night, the voice, the deep boom and monotone of its need. She thought of the cypress trees, like great silver candlesticks in an enchanted wood. She thought of the swamp water, white as a snowfield, though there was no snow, of course, not even in winter. She thought of the rising mist, like the liquid air of this courtroom, and the silence and impossible solitude.

Solon Gregg sat in his chair, in the steaming intensity of hatred and body odor and old fear, and with a blast of hatred and ancient rage at his father for his sister's rape and for everything else he ever lost or feared, with the glare he directed towards the old colored man up on the witness stand, he dared Uncle to point a finger at him.

Alice watched the parrot make its third, its final circle around the courtroom, hopeless beast, world-weary bird. She thought of Jeeter Skeeter, the little Indian boy who could sometimes not speak to Alice at the end of a day, or even look at her, but could only walk around and around her chair, where she sat, as if to weave some magic spell of gratitude and love, or maybe of disbelief that good things are real.

She thought of Dr. Dust, and of Kubla Khan. She called

out loud to the parrot from her balcony roost: "Weave a circle round him thrice, for he on honeydew hath fed, and drunk the milk of Paradise," and even as she chanted this magic charm, she knew it did not apply to the murderer around whom the circle was woven, unless all magic was black to the core and there was no difference between murder and the poetry of owling with your father, and this she could not accept.

The children in the front row of the balcony called out after her, in unison: "Weave a circle round him thrice!" It was their favorite poem. Don't leave us, Alice, don't ever leave us in our narrow coffin of a world without you! "And drunk the milk of Paradise!" they called out to the bird.

The parrot set its wings and began its incredible descent. Down and down, through the liquid atmosphere, the parrot dropped, wingfeathers like a green umbrella, a canopy, a tent so large, so vast, so green that it cast a green shade upon everyone seated in the room, especially Alice and the children, whose lives it changed forever, repaired all damage, and proved the magic of sudden and eternal transformations of the spirit.

To the children the bird was Alice, all in green, their love riding. To Alice the bird was the dead boy. It was Bobo— the magic of good and evil, both.

The parrot landed on Solon Gregg's head. It dug its fine yoke-toed claws into his fire-scarred scalp. For one second it swayed like an eagle on a mountain crag, whipped by strong winds, and then it steadied itself and was firm there.

It shit down Solon's back, great farting blobs of liquid white bird dooky. *White!* it seemed to say, *White, white, white!* It opened its beak as if it had forgotten that it knew no words, and so did not speak, though there was noise that issued forth, more human than animal, before it rang once with its cash register voice, *ching-ching!* and then spoke no more.

With the parrot still standing upon his head, Solon Gregg stood up from his chair and leaned forward upon the table in front of him as though he had no idea that the bird was in the courtroom, let alone upon his own head. The bird was like a strange turban on his head, its big red tail was like a cape down his neck and back.

The scream of villainy and old rage that Solon released from his troubled and violent guts spewed forth from him like spontaneous fires from deep in the Gehenna bowel-pits of the Arrow Catcher garbage dump, flames leaping out, unexpected and dangerous, into peaceful air.

He screamed, "You better not point your nigger motherfucking finger at me, you nigger motherfucker nigger motherfucker motherfucker motherfucker motherfucker! Oh Christ, you goddamn nigger, you better not!"

Judge Swinger pounded his gavel many times.

He said, "Order, order!"

Uncle's arm was no longer heavy, his hand was light as air, lighter, a peaceful, small, floating balloon.

Uncle pointed his finger straight in Solon Gregg's face.

He said, "Thar he."

Thar he, said the echo in Alice's heart. *Thar he. Thar she blows!*

13

DAYS LATER, back at the Arrow Catcher schoolhouse, on
a golden afternoon in late September, when the chalkboards were whistle-clean and every eraser was free of dust,
and the oiled floors smelled like the perfume of fat jungle
flowers after a tropical storm, and after all the witnesses
had all testified down at the courthouse, and the trial was
over, and Bobo's murderers had been set free, as most folks
spected they would be, without apology or logic or shame,
well then, Alice asked her schoolchildren to take out their
big sheets of white butcher paper that Mr. Grady down
at the meat market had so generously donated to their
project, and their paint brushes, and Prang watercolors and
Magic Markers, and to draw pictures, each of them, of
the murder trial, what they remembered most of this horrible travesty of justice, this momentous injustice of setting
child-murderers free, this racial and human insult to each
of them—so Alice said, in her customary way of speaking
her outrage, and so when the children had labored a long
time at their desks and at the art table in the back of the
schoolroom, and were sweaty and paint-covered with exertion and memory and primary colors of paint and horror
and the juices of creation and loss, Alice picked up the

pages that they had bent over for so long and with such industry, and she sorted through them, one by one, and she discovered that each child had drawn a picture of a parrot.

THE DAYS inched on through the autumn, with long, pink sunsets, and then, at night, bright stars, a cooler breeze. Local schools kept their steady schedules, big yellow schoolbuses, study halls, homework, bells to mark beginnings and endings, arrow-catching and football, the marching band.

Fortunata came home from Kosiesko and got her job back as a teacher's aide at the elementary school in Leflore, ten miles away, and so in this way she and Alice had small things to talk about.

Fortunata's younger children were clingy and sweet and tended to cry easily. They followed Fortunata around the house until she had to fuss at them. They pretended to be too sick to go to school so Fortunata would stay home with them.

Alice knew she'd be finding a new place to live soon. She was welcome to stay, Fortunata assured her, but Alice thought there was no reason to stay, now that the children didn't need her, and she wasn't sure she wanted to keep her job at Arrow Catcher Elementary next year, anyway, or even next semester.

Something had changed for Alice, it was hard to say just

what that was. She liked Mr. Archer and did not want to disappoint him, or let him down, but she didn't think she could stay.

She felt responsible, somehow, for failures that were vague to her. In her mind she carried the image in the raindrop and wondered whether there was not more she could have done.

There was something, too, that seemed still unfinished with Dr. Dust, and again she was not sure what. She was still in love with him, of course, and she couldn't live on that forever.

For a while, Runt kept his regular appointment at Red's Goodlookin Bar and Gro., mornings and evenings, too, but something was not the same for him, either. Runt looked for his friend Gilbert Mecklin, the crazy housepainter, but Gilbert was making himself scarce these days.

Even before the trial, Rufus McKay quit singing songs from Hollywood musicals, and stopped sleeping in the shoeshine chair. Then he stopped coming to work altogether. Nobody knew what happened to Rufus McKay.

Somebody said he went to Chicago to find work, he had a sister there. The blues singers stopped showing up at Red's, too, with their boxes and harpoons. All were friends of Rufus McKay's, maybe that had something to do with it. Runt had to admit, he missed them. Their music kept on playing in his head.

One day, down at the Goodlookin Bar and Gro., Runt asked Red to call him Cyrus from now on.

Red thought it was a joke. He thought they were playing a game.

He said, "Okay, Cyrus, and you call me Lance."

Runt said, "No, really."

And so then Red saw that Runt was serious and, after that, he worked hard at calling him Cyrus, but he often slipped and called him Runt, it was going to take him a good while to get the hang of it.

Runt wished he'd followed up on his hunch and found a way out to Runnymede that day, to Uncle's house, it might have changed things. He regretted he hadn't tried harder to find the boy's people.

Some other things happened, too, changes in routine that Runt didn't much care for. A lot of younger men, boys, really, started drinking down at Red's.

They were good customers, and there were a lot of them, as many as ten sometimes, and so Red couldn't very well run them off, business being business and all.

But they were foul-mouthed and unruly and unpredictable and wild, and maybe dangerous. Runt thought so, anyway. Runt didn't much like being around them. These boys didn't seem to have been affected at all by the murder or the trial. It was unsettling to be around people who lived where this thing had happened and for them to seem not to have noticed. There was a little too much of Solon Gregg in every one of these new boys, young men, for Runt's taste.

One time one of these new boys brought a new ax handle with him to Red's Goodlookin Bar and Gro. and dragged a straight-back chair out in the cinder parking lot and stood up on it with the ax handle and said, "Anybody who wants to get hit over the head with an ax handle, line up out here."

Well, hell, who in his right mind would want to get hit over the head with an ax handle, is all Runt wanted to know.

So Runt was pretty astonished when seven or eight of these boys went outside and got in line. This is the way they lived their lives, Runt guessed. Seemed like to Runt you couldn't live this way in a town where this thing had happened.

So they lined up, these new boys. Each one took his turn. The boy on the chair hauled off and cracked each one over the head with the new ax handle, first one, and then the next.

It hurt, too. They seen stars. It like to knocked a couple of the smaller boys out, it hurt so bad. One boy went down on his knees, he couldn't help it. Another one, Crack!— like to paralyzed him. He walked back around and got in line a second time. You figure it out.

Nobody might as well of died at all, no murderers might as well have got let off, as far as these boys were concerned.

That's the way Runt looked at the whole situation. That's why he didn't like these boys. He didn't trust a man who was not changed by local horror.

Gilbert Mecklin, the housepainter, slacked off in his attendance at Red's Goodlookin Bar and Gro.

This drew some attention.

After a while, he stopped showing up altogether.

Somebody said, "We gone have to mark old Gilbert absent, ain't we?"

Somebody said, "Look like he don't remember his old friends."

Somebody said maybe it was because his boy Sugar found that swole-up body in the spillway, maybe Gilbert couldn't face his friends after that, maybe he was too ashamed and broke-up.

Somebody else said, Well, hail, that didn't make no sense, what kind of sense did that make, it wont logical.

Somebody else said it wont Sugar that found the body no-how, it was Sweet Austin, Gilbert's illegitimate boy with Rosemary Austin, down to the Legion Hut.

Somebody else said that boy wont Gilbert's, Sweet Austin belonged to Morris Austin just sure as I'm standing here, look just like old Morris, and anyway, Gilbert's a family man.

Somebody else said Morris Austin was impotent, that's

why Morris couldn't be Sweet's real daddy, that's what they heard. They said they heard Morris Austin ain't never had a hard-on in his life.

Somebody else said that wont nothing, they said they heard that Miss Alberta, down at the grade school, was born without a vagina.

Some people said, Well, I'll be dog. Is that a fact? Miss Alberta ain't got one? Well, shoot, Miss Alberta and Morris Austin, they ought to get together, go out to a pitcher show.

Somebody else said they heard Gilbert Mecklin had done stopped drinking. Completely quit.

Huh?

What'd you say?

Now wait a minute, let me get this straight. Gilbert Mecklin has done stopped drinking?

That's what they said they heard.

Whoa. Hole up just one durn minute here.

Yep, that's it. Gilbert Mecklin done quit.

The boy with the ax handle mought as well have cracked everybody over the head at once.

Gilbert Mecklin?—are you sho about this? You mean he died, don't you? Seem like that would be a more likely explanation.

Red said, "Gilbert ain't quit drinking. That's all there is to it."

Somebody said, "That ain't what I heard."

Red said, "It ain't. Gilbert's too good a friend. Gilbert wouldn't do that to me."

Somebody said, "Well, I wouldn't take it too durn personal, Red."

Red wagged his head. He wouldn't look anybody in the eye.

He jerked out his handkerchief from his back pocket, a big red bandanna, and blew his nose angrily into it.

The place fell quiet for a time.

Now here was the problem with the new boys.

One of them said, "He goes to them Don't Drink meetings, what I heard."

Everybody looked at the new boy.

Why don't you just shit right in the middle of your dinner plate, while you're at it, son?

Red laid the bandanna down on the counter.

He took a deep breath.

He reached up under the counter and took the enormous pistol from where it lay beside the Kotex.

He raised the pistol, level out in front of him, and held it on the boy.

The boy took a step backwards and froze.

Real slow, Red said, "Get your goddamn ass, out'n my goddamn store, or I'll blow your goddamn head off."

The boy started walking backwards, slow, till he reached

the door, and then he pushed open the two screened doors with his back, without taking his eyes off Red, and then turned quickly and took off running, and disappeared, down the steps, through the cinder lot, and he was gone.

Red dropped the pistol onto the floor, and it clattered like pots and pans. He put his head down on the counter and wept.

He said, "It's all over, boys, the world is coming to an end."

Somebody said, "No, it ain't, Red, come on now, boy, it truly ain't."

Red said, "It ain't no use, there ain't no comfort in the land."

Runt said, "I got to be going, Red. You take care of yourself, you hear?"

Somebody said, "Get a grip, Red, you can do it, that's all right, you get a grip."

Runt slipped on out of the store.

He thought, Gilbert Mecklin has done quit drinking?— goes to Don't Drink meetings? Now ain't that the limit?

He thought, And Red!—Law, have mercy, did you ever see such a durn sight in your life?—that boy was a mess in this world, now wont he, that Red.

Coach Wily Heard, the one-legged arrow-catching coach, had been having a taste with the boys that autumn day. He followed Runt out of the store.

Coach Heard hadn't been able to get Runt's boy out of his mind, Roy Dale. It wasn't like Roy Dale to shoot a classmate in the head. If it had been anybody but Smoky Viner, the situation could have been dangerous.

When Coach Heard had a few drinks in him, he took an interest in his students.

He called out, "Hey, Runt, hole up."

Runt stopped at the bottom of the porch steps and looked back.

Coach said, "Can I talk to you a minute, Runt?"

Runt said, "Call me Cyrus."

Coach said, "Oh, yeah, right. Sure thing, Cyrus."

Coach said, "How's your boy, Cyrus, how's Roy Dale getting along these days?"

Runt said, "Well, you know."

Coach said, "Yeah, I know."

They kept on walking across the cinder lot.

Coach said, "How about I give you a ride home, Runt. I got my pickup parked right out yonder by the hell-hound shed."

Runt said, "Well, sure, Coach, that'd be nice, thank you. Call me Cyrus."

Coach said, "Cyrus, right."

They walked over and climbed up in the pickup. Runt slammed his door shut, and then Coach Heard pumped the accelerator a couple of times with his fiberglass foot and started up the engine.

Runt said, "You're not wearing your peg leg today, I see."

Coach said, "I got it slung back in the bed of the truck if I need it. My wife prefers for me to wear the one with a foot."

Runt said, "It's a little dressier."

Coach said, "I suppose."

Runt said, "Your shoes wear out more or less even, too, I'd guess."

Coach said, "I guess."

Coach drove on past the gin, out towards the edge of Balance Due.

Coach said, "Runt, I been concerned about your boy."

Runt said, "Call me Cyrus."

Coach said, "Cyrus, right."

Runt said, "He's mad at the world, ain't no doubt about that."

Coach said, "I'm fond of that boy, Runt, I'm not going to lie to you."

Runt said, "Call me Cyrus."

Coach said, "So you're saying you want me to call you Cyrus, is that it? Do I understand you correctly?"

Runt said, "I'd appreciate it."

Coach said, "Cyrus it is, then. You got it. No problem."

They pulled up in front of Runt's house. The truck came banging to a halt. The leg in the bed came sliding from the tailgate up to the cab.

Coach Heard opened up the glove compartment and took out a nipper, actually an army canteen, dented metal with a stained canvas cover. The cover was army green and had the initials US stamped beneath the snaps.

Coach said, "You want a little taste before you go in the house, Runt?"

Coach unscrewed the cap and took a swig of the whiskey he had stashed there in the canteen. He made a face like, oh yes!

Runt said, "Call me Cyrus."

Coach said, "I did call you Cyrus. That is what I called you."

Runt said, "No, it wont, but it's okay, just call me Cyrus from now on."

Coach said, "I could have sworn I called you Cyrus."

Runt said, "No."

He took the canteen from Coach, and held it in his hands.

Coach said, "Well, okay, have it your way, but I still think I called you Cyrus. I'm pretty sure I did."

Runt looked hard at the canteen. He raised it up to his lips and took a taste from it. He thought about Gilbert Mecklin at the Don't Drink meetings. Wonder what they do there? He took another taste, a bigger taste this time.

He said, "Uh."

Coach said, "I picked up that canteen down at Swami Don's Elegant Junk."

He screwed the cap back on and put the canteen back in the glove compartment. It was a nice roomy glove compartment, one of the things Coach admired about a GMC.

Runt said, "Well, it's a good one, all right. World War II, it looks like."

Coach said, "That'd be my guess. I don't have nothing left of my army gear. Uniforms, nothing."

Runt said, "Is that right."

Coach said, "After I lost my leg, it just made me sick to look at it, all them reminders. I threw it all away."

Runt said, "Well—"

Coach said, "Now I miss it, though. I wish I had it back. All that stuff. Helmet, liner, fatigues, boots, green underwear, all of it."

Runt said, "Come on in the house for a while."

They walked up on the porch and into the house.

Runt said, "Sit down. Take that chair, there by the window."

Coach said, "First aid kit, entrenching tool, C-rats, rain gear, gas mask. I threw it all away, I was in so much pain. Heart pain, you know. My leg hurt pretty goddurn bad too. I wish I had all of it back now."

Runt said, "But you're picking up some spare pieces, are you?—like the canteen? Replacing it as well as you can?"

Coach said, "You know, Runt, I didn't come here to talk about getting my leg shot off."

Runt said, "Call me Cyrus."

Coach said, "Goddammit, Runt! I did call you Cyrus! Goddamn, man! I been calling you Cyrus till I'm blue in the goddamn face!"

Fortunata came in the room then.

She said, "Don't get up, keep your seats."

Neither man had moved.

When she said this, though, Coach Heard began to struggle to lift himself out of the sagging chair that he was collapsed into. His false leg had gotten stuck out in a funny direction, and he couldn't get a grip on the floor with his plastic foot.

Fortunata said, "Really, just passing through, keep your seat."

She touched Runt on the shoulders as she passed his chair, and went on out the door.

She said, "See you later, Cyrus."

Runt said, "I'm thinking about meeting a friend somewhere tonight."

When he said this, Fortunata stuck her head back in the door.

She said, "A friend?"

He said, "Well, yeah."

She said, "Who?"

He said, "Just a friend I ain't seen for a while."

She said, "Well—"

He said, "I was thinking I might meet Gilbert Mecklin tonight."

She said, "Gilbert Mecklin?"

He said, "Well, yeah."

She said, "Well, okay."

He said, "All right."

She said, "Down at Red's?"

He said, "No, a different place."

She said, "A different place?"

He said, "I'll talk to you about it."

She said, "Well. Okay."

When she was gone, Coach said, "You're a lucky man, Runt."

Runt just looked at him.

Coach said, "What? What are you looking at."

Runt said, "Call me Cyrus."

Coach said, "You sawed-off little motherfucker! If you say that to me one more time—"

They sat for a while without speaking. Coach finally cooled down a little.

He looked up and saw the parrot in its cage.

He said, "Is that the same parrot you won in a fistfight?"

Runt said, "Same old parrot, yeah."

Coach said, "You ain't got a little taste of something in the house, have you, Cyrus, by any chance?"

Runt said, "Naw, sho don't."

Coach said, "Does he still make that noise like a cash register?"

Runt said, "Oh yeah, still ringing."

Coach chuckled. He said, "Still ringing." He took a breath and let it out.

Coach said, "I could go out to the truck and bring in that canteen."

Runt said, "You could do that. That'd be all right."

Coach didn't move. He just kept sitting there.

Coach said, "It ain't the same, trying to replace all that stuff."

Runt said, "I guess not."

Coach said, "I think somebody had done peed in the canteen. It smelled pretty stout when I bought it."

Runt said, "I didn't notice nothing in the flavor."

Coach said, "I wrenched it out."

Runt said, "Uh-huh."

Coach said, "Some people, boy like Roy Dale, for example, even a sweet boy like that, a murder like this can put a mean streak in them."

Runt said, "Uh-huh."

Coach said, "Murder ain't no good for nobody."

Runt said, "Well—"

Coach said, "Puts us in mind of what we ain't got."

Runt said, "Roy Dale missed his mama. Ain't said one kind word to her since she got back."

Coach said, "I ain't got no children, Runt. Ain't got no leg."

Runt said, "Call me Cyrus."

Coach said, "Ain't got my army gear, even. I threw my medals away. I threw away a Purple Heart and a Silver Star. Can you beat that? That's how much pain was in my heart. What's my life amount to, Runt? I'm finishing up my life by drinking whiskey out of a canteen some stranger done pissed in."

Runt said, "Uh, well, Coach, I hate to harp on this, you know, it might seem like a small point to you, but I swear I think I could hear your problems a lot better if you could call me Cyrus. I wish you'd give it a try."

Coach said, "What I'm trying to say to you is, I never knowed about this emptiness inside me, until that little colored boy got killed and Solon and Dexter got let loose. That's when it come to me. I want them uniforms back, and them brass belt buckles, them cartridge belts and Eisenhower caps and field jackets. I want my daddy, who died twenty years ago. I want every durn thing I ever lost."

Runt said, "I'm trying to do better, Coach. I'm trying to give Roy Dale back some of what I took away."

Coach said, "You'll never be able to make it up to him. What's gone is gone forever."

Runt said, "I know. I think I know that."

Coach said, "He's a good boy, Roy Dale is. I hope this murder don't kill him."

Runt said, "Well—"

Coach said, "Why did they let them loose? Everybody knowed they was guilty."

Runt said, "I don't know. I wish I knew."

Coach said, "Would you have let them go, Runt?—if you had been on the jury?"

Runt took a breath and let it out.

The parrot rustled in his cage. He banged his big strong green wings against the wire bars.

The parrot rang like a cash register.

The parrot said, "I love you!"

The parrot said, "Pussy is good!"

The parrot said, "Ree-pul-seevo!"

The parrot said, "We are all alone!"

The parrot said, "Call me Cyrus!"

Coach said, "Jesus Christ! You been working with that parrot some, ain't you?"

Runt said, "It takes a while."

Coach said, "It seems like it's worth it. That's a mighty fine parrot."

Runt said, "Fortunata's allergic to it, though. We're talking about trying to find the old feller a good home."

Coach said, "You're having to get rid of your parrot? Just when you've got his engine running good?"

Runt said, "It'd be nice if we could keep him."

Coach said, "I'd hate for you to give up your parrot, sholy would."

Runt said, "It ain't good for the wife, you know how that is. Affects her breathing."

Coach said, "Well—"

Runt said, "They ain't a big market for parrots, you can imagine."

Coach said, "Well, shoot, I wouldn't mind having me a parrot."

Runt said, "You want a parrot?"

Coach said, "Well, yeah, hell yeah. I'd love to have me a good parrot. I always wanted me a parrot. That or a ventriloquist's dummy. I'd be willing to pay top dollar for a good parrot."

Runt said, "I'd have to talk it over with the wife, you know. We'd have to say something to the children."

Coach said, "No pressure, Cyrus, no pressure at all! And the chaps can come over and play with it anytime they want to. Visiting privileges, you know."

Runt said, "What do you want with a parrot?"

Coach said, "I don't know. I already got me a peg leg. Seem like all I need now is a parrot."

Runt said, "You gone sail the high seas, ain't you, Coach."

Coach said, "I'm gone get me a Jolly Roger."

Runt said, "It's a bad world, Coach. It's an evil world we live in."

Coach said, "I know, Cyrus. I know. We'll just have to make do."

14

IN JUNE, on the last day of school, when Alice's first year of teaching was finished, Mr. Archer, the principal, stopped by Alice's classroom and begged Alice to stay on, at least one more year, the school would absolutely go under without her, he said. Alice told him she was sorry, she had already made her mind up, she was moving on, it was the best thing.

She continued packing up her belongings into cardboard boxes.

Mr. Archer said, "We really need you here, Alice."

Alice said, "You've been wonderful to me."

Mr. Archer turned sideways in the doorway and leaned against the frame.

He said, "Is it some boy who is stealing you away from us?"

Alice smiled, thinking of Dr. Dust.

She said, "No, it's not a boy."

Mr. Archer kept standing in the doorway of her classroom and picked absentmindedly at his scalp, and then examined his bloody fingernail.

Alice moved quietly through the schoolroom. She picked up paper off the floor. She straightened the desks.

Mr. Archer said, "You needn't bother with that, Alice."
She said, "Well, I don't mind."

She removed the thumbtacks from the bulletin board that held the children's dental hygiene charts. Glenn Gregg's name tag was still among them, it had not been removed, so she took it down as well, and placed it on her desk in a neat stack with the others. The same with the name tag on Glenn's desk, and his cloakroom hook, and his boot bin.

Mr. Archer came in the room, sat in one of the low desks, and turned his knees out to the side so he would fit.

He said, "These things happen, Alice."

She said, "I know."

He said, "People die. Children die."

She said, "Well, anyway."

He said, "Yeah."

They were silent together for a while.

Alice was afraid Mr. Archer was going to try to talk to her from his heart, so she said, "These are the cumulative reading scores and the math booklets." She pointed to two stacks of manila envelopes and folders.

He said, "Just leave them there, on the desk."

She said, "Do you want these windows pulled down?"

Mr. Archer said, "Alice—"

Alice said, "Don't say it, Mr. Archer."

She was afraid he was going to tell her he loved her. She said, "I was in love with my college professor when I moved here. I guess I still am in love with him."

He said, "I wondered if there was someone in your life."

She said, "Just him."

He said, "Well—"

She said, "Anyway—"

He said, "Anyway—"

She said, "Good-bye, Mr. Archer. You're a very nice man."

He said, "I wish I could stop picking at my scalp."

She laughed, and so then Mr. Archer laughed, too.

Alice examined her hands for dust.

Mr. Archer said, "I can put those boxes in the trunk of your car for you."

Alice said, "I'm on foot, as usual."

He said, "Oh, right, of course."

She said, "Uncle Runt will pick them up later."

He said, "If you'd like, I could—"

She said, "No, really."

He said, "Well—"

Mr. Archer stood up from the little desk.

He said, "You have a very creative mind, you know."

She said, "Thank you."

He said, "Well—"

She extended her hand to him. For a moment he looked at her hand as if it were in a display case, and then he quickly took it and gave it a firm handshake and released it.

She said, "Good-bye."

He said, "Yes, and, well, best of luck."

School was out. Alice breathed a sweetness of DDT in the sun-drenched Delta air. The school year was finished. Glenn Gregg was dead. Bobo was dead. Alice walked out of the schoolhouse into the June sun, full summer in Mississippi. She left her belongings behind.

Alice was walking now, she didn't know where. She didn't want to go home yet, to Uncle Runt's house. She had not learned to call him Uncle Cyrus yet, and he did not ask her to. She felt sweat collecting in the small of her back, beneath her blouse. She walked a long distance around town.

She laid eyes on everything, as she had laid her hands a final time on the desks, the children's workbooks. Shanker's Drug Store; the water tower; the fish camp where the body had been pulled to, behind a motorboat; the Legion Hut with its World War II cannon; the statue of the Confederate soldier looking south; men in overalls spitting into lard cans; the Arrow Hotel, with its tree-shaded veranda, but with Miz Peebuddy out of sight.

Arrow Catcher was empty now, no reporters on the courthouse lawn, no sightseers in the Arrow Cafe.

She walked out on the Roebuck bridge and leaned on the wooden railing and looked down at a line of turtles sunning on a log. With her toe she raked a couple of pieces of loose gravel off the bridge and watched them fall down into the water. They hit and sent wide ripples outward for a long distance.

She left the bridge and walked past the empty fairgrounds, the site of the annual Arrow-Catcher Fair. She walked past the house where the gospel singer died, and past the frozen meat locker where the Pentecostal revival was held. She walked past Harper's woods, where a one-man band had played for pennies, an accordion, and cymbals on his knees, and a harmonica on a head frame, and an oogah-horn on his belt. On the street where she walked, she watched the ice man, asleep on the ice wagon, as two blind mules pulled him through town with water pouring out of the bed of the wagon, hundred-pound blocks of ice melting beneath canvas tarpaulins. She saw the house that had been visited by a sin-eater, and a corner where a Chinese yo-yo man named Yo had peddled his wares.

When she reached her destination, she knew it was where she had been going all along. She had walked past the colored cemetery, which made her think of Bobo, though he was not buried there, his mama had taken him back to Chicago, and she had kept on walking, past St. George-by-the-Lake, and finally she had walked so far, almost all the way out to Highway 49, that her feet hurt and she had become sweaty in the heat. She was standing outside of Swami Don's Elegant Junk.

Parked outside the junk store, in the gravelled parking lot, was a big white Cadillac, the car that belonged to Sally Anne Montberclair.

Sally Anne was browsing in Swami Don's when Alice walked through the door. She looked up and smiled at Alice and spoke to her as if they knew each other.

Sally Anne had taken a pasteboard guitar, with rotted gut strings, down from a wall hook, where it had hung beside several sweat-stained leather horse collars and a rusted plowshare and a Confederate sword.

She said, "Swami Don claims this is Robert Johnson's first guitar. Do you believe him?"

Alice said, "Robert who?"

Sally Anne said, "Oh, well, it doesn't matter." She placed the guitar on the wall hook again.

Alice didn't know what else to say. She recognized Sally Anne, of course. She liked her at the trial, or believed she would like her if she knew her. You could tell she was a good person. Alice wished she hadn't been so ignorant when Sally Anne tried to make conversation about the guitar.

Alice said, "This is some store."

Sally Anne said, "It ought to be listed in Cook's Tour Guide."

Alice said, "In what?"

Sally Anne said, "You know, a guide for tourists."

Alice said, "Oh."

Alice turned away and moved along one of the narrow, crowded aisles of the store. Sally Anne moved along another aisle. Alice could see her, sort of, through the empty spaces between junk.

Alice seemed to be standing in the iron section. The iron section, for heaven's sake! Could there be a less interesting section of the junk store? What would Sally Anne think of her?

There were iron skillets of all shapes and sizes (including one in the shape of Mississippi); farm implements, scythes and disks and plows and a pecan separator; irons for ironing; iron anchors for boats; a steam radiator; iron pipes of all lengths; a cannonball; a small cannon barrel; iron wagon wheels; iron hitching posts, with the tops shaped like the heads of horses; an iron pickaninny wearing livery; fire irons from a fireplace; leg irons from a prison; a weight-lifting set from a gymnasium; an Iron Maiden, from a torture chamber; a chastity belt from God-knows-where, with a handprinted sign that said LOST KEY; a cast-iron coffin with MADE IN PITTSBURGH stamped into the lid; an iron statue of a snarling dog that made Alice jump; an iron coupling from a train caboose—it must have weighed a ton!

Through the shelves she could see Sally Anne, browsing, a few feet away. Alice said, "This is just iron."

Sally Anne said, "My aisle is not much better."

Alice said, "What's your aisle?"

Sally Anne said, "Well, it's hard to say. Come look."

Alice walked down to the end of the long iron aisle, and looped around into the space where Sally Anne was standing.

She said, "I'm Alice."

Sally Anne said, "I saw you at the trial. I'm Sally Anne. I'm—well, I guess you know who I am, I guess you couldn't miss me, could you?"

Alice said, "The murderer's wife."

Sally Anne turned to look at the junk in her aisle.

She said, "This aisle seems to be magic stuff." She picked up a walking cane and it popped out into a bouquet of fake flowers.

Alice said, "I'm sorry. I shouldn't have said that. I don't know what gets into me sometimes."

She said, "Dexter is gone, I don't even know where. The house is up for sale. I'm going to go away, too."

Alice said, "Magic stuff?"

Sally Anne said, "Well, I'm not sure. Look at this."

There were endless stacks of Tarot cards, maybe a thousand decks altogether, some new and still wrapped in cellophane, others so battered and greasy you could hardly make out the figures.

Sally Anne said, "Swami Don must have hit the Tarot jackpot."

Alice said, "The Tarot truck must have wrecked out on Highway 49."

Sally Anne said, "There must have been a good Tarot crop last year."

Alice said, "Swami Don buys his Tarot cards by the pound."

The two women laughed together. They said, "Shh. Swami Don is around here somewhere." They laughed some more. They said, "Shh, shh."

They walked along together.

There was a steamer trunk filled with magic wands, and a set of leather saddlebags with more magic wands, sticking out of both sides.

Alice said, "I saw a yellow dog dragging a saddlebag full of harmonicas down in Balance Due the day of the murder."

For a while neither woman said anything. Alice started to be sorry she said this.

Then Sally Anne said, "That dog must have been browsing in the music section of Swami Don's store."

They were able to smile again.

There was a long shelf filled with nothing but silk top

hats with white rabbits poking their heads out. Sally Anne said, "They're so *cute*." There was a wooden crate filled with joined steel rings. Alice picked up a handful of the rings, and they all separated and fell apart with a clatter. Alice said, "Yikes." There was another crate, very large, marked FLY NG CARPETS DO NOT OPEN. The two women looked at one another and rolled their eyes. There were stacks of neatly folded silk scarves, and another large stack of magic capes, and cigar boxes filled with talismans of various descriptions, and several pairs of Seven League Boots, clearly marked. There were turbans and tea leaves and wall charts with diagrams of open palms. There were signboards with red palms and others with silhouettes of Indian maidens. There was a wooden barrel, and when Alice lifted the lid, she saw a nest of writhing green snakes.

Swami Don, sitting up near the cash register, must have heard Alice slam the lid. He said, "Nonpoisonous, nothing to worry about."

Alice whispered, "This beats iron, anyway."

Sally Anne said, "I always wanted to come down here, since I was a little girl."

Alice said, "Why didn't you?"

Sally Anne said, "It was considered tacky."

Alice thought about this. She said, "I guess that's the one advantage of coming from white trash. 'Tacky' really never comes up."

She said this thoughtfully.

Sally Anne said, "I figure, once you become a murderer's wife, you gain pretty much the same advantage."

Alice thought about this, too. She liked Sally Anne. She had known she would.

Alice said, "Well, now, that's a nice way of looking at it."

Sally Anne said, "I suppose."

Swami Don's Elegant Junk was huge, much larger than it appeared on the outside. Alice and Sally Anne looked at boxes for disappearances, and boxes for sawing women in half, and boxes with slits for swords.

Alice said, "I saw Bobo's body in a raindrop."

Sally Anne looked at her.

She said, "In a raindrop?"

Alice said, "I was walking home from school on the day of the murder—you remember how it rained that day?— and for some unknown reason I happened to look right at a particular raindrop on my coatsleeve and I saw a dead child in the lake."

They moved past bins filled up with disappearing ink and disappearing coins and one large unmarked bin that was completely empty.

Sally Anne said, "Whatever was in this bin seems to have disappeared."

The two women laughed. They moved on down the

aisle, past the magic lanterns, with a sign saying DO NOT TOUCH.

Alice said, "I don't know what to make of any of it."

Sally Anne said, "I've got to try to put it all behind me."

Alice said, "I had never even heard of Bobo. I thought the child in the raindrop was Glenn Gregg, Solon's boy, you know, the child who died during the trial."

Sally Anne said, "How do you mean 'in a raindrop'?"

Alice said, "Like a vision or something. Like a crystal ball."

Sally Anne said, "I don't know what to say. It's all so painful to remember."

Alice said, "Anyway—"

Sally Anne said, "Yeah, anyway—"

They walked on, past the cages full of doves, past the escape tricks, manacles and handcuffs and safes, past the empty tiger cage with heavy iron bars.

Alice said, "This tiger cage ought to be in the iron section, seems like."

Sally Anne said, "Do you, you know, really believe in magic?"

Alice said, "It does seem a little white-trashy, I guess."

Sally Anne said, "No, I didn't mean it like that."

Alice said, "I never thought I did, but I must. That night—you know—"

Sally Anne said, "The night of the murder."

Alice said, "Yeah, well, I had this crazy idea of getting up in the middle of the night and coming down here to Swami Don's and trying to buy a mojo. That's how scared I felt. That's how scared I was. I was willing to try anything."

Sally Anne said, "A what?"

Alice said, "It's a magic charm. Made from a monkey's hand."

Sally Anne said, "A mojo, good Lord."

Alice said, "Maybe I should have tried. I might have found one, judging from all this junk."

Sally Anne said, "We could ask Swami Don if he has one."

The two women smiled together.

Alice said, "Hm."

They came to a box full of small, bleached-out bones and tiny skulls. The sign said BLACK CATS MIX AND MATCH.

They came to a blue garment of some kind. The sign said ASTRAL FLIGHT COVERLET.

The women shrugged. You crawl under it, maybe, and pop up on another planet, who knows.

They came to a red flannel bag that smelled of oils and spices. The sign said JOHN THE CONQUEROO.

They came to a crystal ball.

Here they stopped.

The ball was pure and clear, about the size of a perfectly round canteloupe. There was only one ball, although most everything else in the store seemed to have been stocked by the gross. The crystal sat on the shelf in a low brass stand.

Alice and Sally Anne stood there, looking at it, into it. They could see nothing, nothing at all.

They continued to walk together through the store. They browsed, they spoke in low voices. They spoke, finally, from their hearts. Maybe, finally, they did weep together, and maybe held each other tight. Nobody but Bobo knows for sure what happened next, but maybe, behind Alice and Sally Anne, the crystal ball in Swami Don's Elegant Junk shone with the bright blue light of empty interiors and of faraway and friendly stars and all their hopeful planets and golden moons.